LITTLE SISTER

(Cleo's Story – a companion novel to *Been So Long*)

Adrienne Thompson

Pink Cashmere Publishing Co.

USA

Edited by Alyndria Mooney

Cover Design by Adrienne Thompson

Cover Art from dreamstime.com

Printed in the United States of America

First Printing 2013

ISBN: 0988871319

ISBN-13: 978-0-9888713-1-1

Also by Adrienne Thompson

Bluesday

Lovely Blues (Bluesday Book II)

Been So Long

When You've Been Blessed (Feels Like Heaven)

See Me

Coming Soon:

Rapture (A Been So Long Prequel) – This book will be available
exclusively on my website as a FREE read

Been So Long 2 (Body and Soul)

As always, thank You, Lord, for blessing me beyond measure.

To my readers: I thank God for you. Know that you are truly appreciated.

Love is patient, love is kind...

1 Corinthians 13:4 NIV

SOUNDTRACK BY MARY J. BLIGE

"My Life"

"Keep Your Head"

"Baggage"

"Memories"

"Where I've Been"

"Good Woman Down"

"In The Morning"

"Fade Away"

"Fly Away"

"The Living Proof"

"Real Love"

"You Remind Me"

"Midnight Drive"

"Searching"

"Hurt Again"

"Not Lookin'"

"He Think I Don't Know"

"Let No Man Put Asunder"

"Testimony"

"Be Happy"

"Shake Down"

"Mr. Wrong"

"Irreversible"

"Just Fine"

"The next day, I felt a constant uneasiness. The dream had awakened memories that played over and over in my mind. For the first time in years, I wondered about my little sister. Cleo had run away when she was only twelve. I was sixteen at the time. I'd tried my best to shield her from our mother's abuse. I'd tried to take care of her, but she'd left anyway."

"I probably would have left too, but by then, I'd met Corey, and his friendship had given me a reason to stick around. I wondered where Cleo was or if she was even still alive…"

—Mona-Lisa Dandridge from Been So Long

PROLOGUE

1993

US HIGHWAY 67 SOUTH—NEAR SEARCY, ARKANSAS

I crouched over the toilet in the grimy gas station restroom, trying to keep my balance as I relieved myself. I eyed the graffiti-riddled stall walls and door, reading the various markings. "Wherever you go, there you are"…"Jill was here"…"Jesus is love"…"kiss my—" well, you get the gist of it. After I finished, I stepped out of the stall to the sink, where I washed my hands and dried them on my jeans— no paper towels, no hand drier. I pushed the door open and walked back out into the station. The aroma of old fried chicken and old chicken grease filled my nose. I eyed the food in the warmer, and although the chicken looked dry—almost petrified, I longed for a piece.

I reached into my pocket and pulled out the twenty dollars I took from my mother's purse. I'd been walking the highway for hours. All I had for breakfast was a pop tart and some orange juice. I skipped lunch altogether, so that dry chicken seemed more like a huge slice of greasy pepperoni pizza to me.

I ordered a two-piece meal and slid onto one of the two benches situated in what amounted to the convenience store's restaurant. I was so hungry and so engrossed with filling my stomach, that I didn't even notice that the man sitting across from me was staring at me. All I cared about was the leg and thigh that I had drenched with hot sauce. I took a big bite and nearly swallowed the meat without chewing it. I took a gulp of orange soda before finishing the chicken leg in two more bites.

I was entranced with eating the old chicken, stale roll, and rock-hard okra—transfixed with the satisfying fullness that I felt. I sat there and licked my fingertips before polishing off my soda. I stood from the bench and rubbed my hands on the thighs of my jeans. As I headed out of the gas station, my legs felt as heavy as my eyelids. My full belly had zonked my energy, and as I continued my hours-long trek down the highway towards nowhere in particular, I moved much slower than I had at the beginning of my journey.

At twilight, I started to think about finding somewhere to sleep for the first time that day. I had not planned things out too well, and now, as I walked along the shoulder of Highway 67, the increasing darkness began to frighten me. I glanced towards the dense trees that lined the highway and my imagination began to see glowing eyes in the darkness. What if there was a bear or a werewolf in there? What if there was an ax murderer hiding out in the woods?

I pulled my thin windbreaker around my body and rubbed my hands up and down my arms as the evening air began to chill me. I had to figure out some place to sleep. I shoved my hand into the hip pocket of my jeans and felt the fifteen dollars I had left. That, along with a backpack full of Cheetos, Pop Tarts, and oranges, was all I had with me. Well, and the three outfits I had packed.

I was so deep in thought that I didn't hear the truck when it pulled to a stop on the shoulder. By now I was used to the noise of the highway, the sound of cars whizzing by or the loud horns of the big rigs, so a truck braking behind me didn't concern me. I continued to walk and ponder my situation when I heard a man's voice behind me.

"Hey, little sister! Where you headed?!"

I frowned but I didn't turn around. He couldn't have been speaking to me.

"Hey, little girl!"

I stopped in my tracks and turned around. I didn't answer him because I still wasn't sure if he was talking to me. The voice came from the man I'd seen at the gas station. The one who was sitting across from me. He was tall with skin the color of potting soil. His hair was cut in a neat fade. He wore wrinkled jeans and a blue flannel shirt. He raised his thick eyebrows, smiled, and repeated himself. "Where you going?"

I shrugged.

"You don't know?"

I shrugged again. I remembered my grandmother telling me not to never talk to strangers. That was before she moved away, but I still remembered it. I remembered everything she ever told me. This man was a stranger, so I wasn't about to talk to him.

"Can't talk?" he asked.

I just stood there and looked at him.

"Wanna ride? It's getting dark out here. Ain't safe for a pretty little girl to be walking down the highway in the dark."

"I'm alright," I finally said then I turned and resumed my trek.

"It's wild dogs in them woods. You sure you wanna keep walking out here all by yourself?"

I froze. Wild dogs? Now that made my ears stand at attention. If he was telling the truth, I'd have no way to fight them off.

"Look, I can give you a ride if you want."

My eyes darted from the woods back to the man's face. He was smiling as he nodded towards the huge rig that sat behind him on the shoulder. He was a stranger, but he seemed nice enough, and I didn't want to deal with any dogs or werewolves, for that matter.

So I said, "Okay."

"Where you headed?" he asked.

"Um…to my daddy's house?" I really wanted to find my grandmother, but I had no idea where she lived. My mother never told me where she went after she left Arkansas. But she'd once told *me where my father lived. I figured I'd take my chances with him. He couldn't be any worse than my mother.*

"Where he live?"

"Milwaukee, I think."

The man nodded. "All right."

He helped me climb into his big truck. Then he climbed into the driver's seat and said, "Buckle up."

I did as I was told and watched as he reached behind my seat for something. He pulled out a big bag of Doritos and a can of soda and handed them both to me. I smiled as I ripped the bag open.

"What's your name, little sister?" he asked.

"Cleo."

"Cleo? That's a funny name for a little girl."

"It's short for Cleopatra."

He nodded. "Oh, I see. Well, Cleo, I'm Frank. How old are you?"

"Twelve," I said as I bit down on a chip. "How old are you?"

He laughed. "I'm twenty-six. Look, I'm heading to Memphis. After that, you're on your own."

I nodded. "Okay."

Frank turned the volume up on the radio. A Mary J. Blige song blared from the speakers as he pulled his rig back onto the highway. I rested my head against the back of the seat and eyed the dirty truck cab. There were chip sacks and soda cans all over the floor. In the ashtray, I saw some greenish-brown grass and some cigarette papers. It was the same stuff my mama and her friends were always smoking. I looked over at Frank who was singing along with the music while tapping his fingers on the steering wheel.

"Thank you," I said softly.

He looked over at me and smiled. "No problem, little sister."

We were quiet for a few seconds and then he said, "You know, if you stick with me, I'll take care of you. A lot of bad things can happen to you out here on this road. It's some bad people out here."

"It's some bad people at home, too," I said.

He frowned as he glanced over at me. "Somebody hurt you?"

I nodded slowly.

"Somebody hurt me, too, when I was about your age—one of my mama's friends."

"Really?"

"Yeah."

I felt relieved. There was someone else who knew what I'd been through. I closed my eyes and before I knew it, I'd drifted off to sleep.

1

"My Life"

2011

159 Shady Grove Road, Crittenden County, Arkansas—near West Memphis

The day I received the call, I was in my little office at the rear of my home. I was pouring over the next week's schedule. What started as a volunteer counseling service I spearheaded at my church had grown by leaps and bounds. Now I was entrusted with handling not only the day to day operations of a full-time counseling center, but I was also over the church's women's homeless shelters. The week ahead was full of appointments and obligations, and I loved it.

On that day, when the call came, I was happy in my home. Happy with the life I'd managed to create. But all of that would soon come crumbling down around me.

"Hello?" I said as I continued to study my schedule. I didn't recognize the number on the caller ID, but that was nothing new. People were always calling for information or trying to get placed in one of the shelters.

"Hello, is this Gina Williams-Grant?" the caller asked.

I held the phone for a moment. Something about the voice halted me. It was vaguely familiar and that bothered me. "Yes. Who is this?" I questioned.

"My name is Mona-Lisa Dandridge. I'm looking for my sister. Her name was Cleo Williams. I was wondering if maybe you knew or heard of her."

I held the phone loosely, feeling a combination of shock and bewilderment and fear. This woman had uttered a name I hadn't heard in years—my *real* name. And she said she was my sister. *My sister?* Could the voice on the other end really belong to my sister? But why after all these years? After all the years I'd hoped and prayed she'd find me. After all the times I'd searched the web for any proof that she or my mother had looked for me and found none. And now, so many years later, a lifetime really, she was calling me?

All these thoughts cluttered my mind as the woman on the other end, the woman who said she was my sister and claimed to be looking for me, waited for my reply. But my voice was caught in my throat. I couldn't speak and if I could, what would I say?

"H…hello? Are you still there?" the woman asked. The phone was now under my ear and I barely heard her uncertain voice.

I choked back tears as I said, "I don't know a Cleo Williams. I'm sorry I couldn't help you."

Then I hung up the phone and stared at it with many thoughts running through my mind. *Troubling thoughts.* I continued to wonder if the woman really was my sister. And if so, how did she find me? But most importantly, if she could find me, what was to keep *him* from finding me?

2

"KEEP YOUR HEAD"

In mere seconds, the security I'd always felt in my home vanished. I'm not sure how long I sat there staring at the phone, deep in thought. My mind had travelled to a different place and time—a place and time I never wanted to revisit. Memories, *horrible* memories, crowded my mind, leaving room for little else. When I finally shifted my gaze from the phone, I looked down at my hands which rested on the desk in front of me. They were so tightly clenched that my nails were digging into the flesh of my palms. When I opened them, I could see the indentations left behind. I wiped beads of sweat from my brow, and when I stood from my desk, my knees buckled.

What if it was a set-up of some sort? What if he had hired her to call me…whoever she was? What if he'd found me? I walked through my house to the kitchen and peered through the window at my children as they played. My eight-year-old daughter, Serenity, was laughing loudly as she dove into a pile of leaves. Shane, my ten-year-old son, was yelling at her. They were supposed to be raking the leaves, and Shane seemed irritated that she was impeding their progress and jeopardizing the ten dollars their dad had promised to pay each of them.

I watched them and for a moment, things felt normal again. I even allowed a faint smile to creep upon my lips. But it wasn't long before the troubling thoughts returned and with them, a deep sense of panic. What if he was nearby? Our home was surrounded by woods. What if Frank was hiding in the woods, in the thick trees?

I snatched the back door open and screamed, "Kids come in!"

They didn't hear me. They continued to laugh and yell. They had no idea what danger they were in.

"Serenity! Shane! Come in the house! NOW!!!"

This time they both turned to me wearing curious expressions. But they still did not move a muscle.

My patience had run thin at this point, and a rising feeling of dread had wiped out any sense of sanity I was clinging to. I walked outside in my bare feet and grabbed each of my children by the collars of their jackets. "I said, come in this house!"

I drug both of them into the kitchen and slammed then locked the door behind us.

"But we weren't finished!" Serenity whined.

"We would've been if you would've stopped playing around!" Shane countered.

"Whatever, Shane, '*the shame*'!"

"Shut up, Serenity!"

"No, *you* shut up!"

"Both of you shut up!" I screamed.

My two youngest children stood stunned. I'd never raised my voice at them, *ever*. Serenity looked as if she'd burst into tears at any minute. And me? I just stood there frozen. I'd shocked even myself.

"G…go to your rooms," I said softly.

Shane reached for his sister's hand and they both cautiously inched past me, heading out of the kitchen. I collapsed into a chair and stared down at the spotless table. I stared at my reflection in the shiny multicolored tiles. I stared at my round, dark brown eyes, my unruly mess of curly hair, and my full lips. I stared at Gina Williams-Grant, AKA Cleo Williams.

For a moment, I wondered about my oldest son, Aaron, and my husband, Scott. Why had they chosen this weekend to go camping? They were somewhere in the woods surrounding our home. Were they safe? Would Frank find them?

I'd left Frank far behind, or so I thought. But if I was completely honest with myself, Frank was never far from my mind. Neither was the highway where I first met him—where, in a way, he rescued me. He rescued me only to introduce me to horrors I could only imagine. At twelve, I'd run away from my mother's abuse, straight into Frank's trap.

I shook my head. I couldn't go there. I couldn't dwell on what I'd worked so hard to block out. After I left Frank, I'd never spoken of him again. He was Aaron's father, but Aaron was so small when we left, he didn't even remember him. Scott was the only father he'd known—the only father that mattered.

I stood from the chair and slowly walked up the stairs to my room where I fell into bed and stared at the wall.

3

"BAGGAGE"

I bolted upright in the bed. Sweat soaked the t-shirt and jeans I'd fallen asleep in. Scott sat up beside me and rubbed my shoulder. *When did he make it home?* I wondered.

"You okay?" he said sleepily.

I stared at him for a moment and then said, "When did you get home?"

He yawned. "This afternoon. Shane called and said he and Serenity were hungry. Said you went to bed without fixing any dinner. When Aaron and I made it back, you were knocked out. I figured you must've been pretty tired."

"I...I didn't mean to fall asleep. I...what time is it?"

Scott shrugged. "I dunno. Got to be close to midnight, I guess. You hungry?"

"Has anyone called? Has anyone been here?" I asked, ignoring his question.

Scott turned on a lamp. His green eyes were clouded with concern. "No. You expecting somebody?"

I shook my head. "No, I was just wondering."

"G, the kids said you were upset about something this afternoon.

Serenity said you hollered at them."

"I'm sorry about that. I was just a little on edge. I'm okay now," I said. All Scott knew of my past was that I'd been abused by my mother and then by Aaron's father. I'd never given him the details. I couldn't. It was too painful to share even with a man who loved me more than anyone else in the world ever has.

"Is there something you want to talk about?" he asked as he rubbed his hand up and down my back. "You're soaking wet! Are you sick?"

I shook my head. "N...no."

Scott fixed his eyes on me. "Did you have a nightmare? What was it about, G?" he said knowingly.

"I don't want to talk. Can you just hold me? Just hold me really tight."

He nodded. We lay down and he reached to turn the light off. "Leave it on," I said.

"Okay."

He held me tightly. I closed my eyes and wished I could share the whole truth of my past with this wonderful man. This man who rescued me and my young son when we were on our last leg and our last dime. This man who took me as his wife, flaws and all. Took my son as his and treated him even better than Shane and Serenity, who are his biological children. I should've been able to give him all of me, but I couldn't. I just couldn't.

***

The next morning, I woke up early and cooked a big country breakfast. I felt horrible about Aaron and Scott having to return home early from their camping trip and about yelling at Shane and Serenity. I felt even worse about falling asleep without making them dinner. I hoped that a nice breakfast and a heartfelt apology would at least begin to make up for things.

Serenity was the first to come to the kitchen, her wild sandy hair all over her head. Her round eyes were full of uncertainty as she sat down at the table and softly said, "Good morning, Mama."

"Good morning, Miss Serenity," I said brightly. I walked over to her and hugged her tightly. "I'm sorry for yelling at you yesterday."

She smiled widely. "It's okay, Mama. Are you making cinnamon pancakes?"

"Of course, beautiful. Wanna help?"

She nodded excitedly and followed me to the stove.

A few minutes later, Shane walked into the kitchen and was just as forgiving as his sister. Aaron, I knew, would be a different story. He was fourteen and prone to catch an attitude at a moment's notice. Plus, he'd been looking forward to the camping trip and the time alone with his father for months.

Scott made it downstairs before Aaron did. He kissed me on the cheek and joined Shane at the table where they discussed the day ahead—riding horses, feeding the livestock, and so on. For some reason, Shane loved doing farm chores.

I was loading plates with the big breakfast when Aaron finally made it to the kitchen. He shuffled to the table and slumped into a chair without so much as a word to anyone.

"Good morning, Aaron," I said as I set a plate in front of him.

He picked up his fork and uttered a grumpy "Morning" before digging into his breakfast.

Scott cleared his throat. "We haven't said grace yet, Aaron."

Aaron held the forkful of scrambled eggs in midair for a few seconds before placing it back on the plate. I sat at the table and we all held hands as Scott said grace.

We were all eating quietly when Scott said, "I think I'll go down to the stream and catch us some dinner."

Aaron's eyes lit up. Scott knew what he was doing. Aaron *loved* hunting and fishing. Aaron had his own fishing rod by the time he was five, and he received his own rifle as a birthday gift when he was eight. And he was an excellent marksman—even better than Scott who'd been hunting since he learned to walk.

"Can I go?" Shane asked.

"Sure, how about we head out after we finish up with the chores?" Scott said.

"Dad, can I go?" Aaron asked softly.

"Sure thing. But I think your mom needs to talk to you first. Come on, Shane and Serenity. Let's go take care of the horses."

In just a few seconds, Aaron and I were alone. He kept his eyes glued to the table as I spoke. "Aaron, I'm sorry you had to come home early from your trip. It was my fault but I promise to make it up to you, okay?"

His eyes met mine and his father's face flashed before me. Aaron could've passed for Frank's twin. From the chocolate brown skin, to the deep-set eyes, to the full lips and nose, they were nearly identical.

"It's alright, Mama. Dad told me you were just real tired. We're gonna plan another trip later."

"Okay. Hug?"

Aaron, who stood a whole inch taller than me, hugged me tightly. I smiled. Everything was back to normal.

4

"MEMORIES"

The Life Church Community Outreach Center was located right outside of the West Memphis city limits. It stood right behind the church itself. Next to it was the Life Church Day School. The pastors, who were also my in-laws, lived in a rustic home located in the woods right behind the church. As I pulled to a stop in front of the outreach center, I thought about that day at an Oklahoma diner that I sat huddled in a corner with my three-year-old son, sharing a grilled cheese sandwich and a cup of water with him. It wasn't much, but it was all I could afford. After that meal, I wasn't sure when we'd eat again.

Scott was sitting at the counter with a bunch of other guys. I'd later learn that they'd all travelled to Oklahoma to help repair and paint homes in low income areas. I noticed him right away. Anyone would've noticed him. He was tall and well-built with a deep tan. He had shoulder-length dark hair and piercing green eyes, Yes, I noticed him, but I never thought he'd notice me. As a matter of fact, I was trying not to be noticed—or pitied—by anyone.

To my surprise, just after Aaron and I finished up the last bit of our sandwich, Scott walked over and stood next to our booth.

"Hi," he said with a bright smile.

"H...hi," I stuttered.

"Mind if I sit down with you guys?"

I gave him a curious look as I tried to figure out why in the world he'd want to sit with us. He didn't know us.

Sensing my leeriness, he said, "My name is Scott and I'm from Life Church in Arkansas. I just wondered if I could talk to you for a moment."

Since I was from Arkansas, I was kind of interested in what he had to say, but I still hesitated for a moment. I looked at Aaron who was draining our water glass. Finally I said, "Okay."

Scott sat down and asked, "What's his name?"

"Um, Aaron."

His eyes met mine. "And yours?"

"Uh, Gina," I said, giving him the name I'd adopted after fleeing my abusive lover. But I said the name so softly it sounded like I said "G". Even after I corrected Scott repeatedly, I was always "G" to him.

"Well, G, I want to help you."

I didn't bother to correct him that time, though. "I don't need any help. W...what makes you think I do?" I was kind of insulted. Did I look that bad?

"I can tell." His eyes travelled to the empty plate. It wasn't lost on him that there was only one plate and glass on the table. Then his gaze rested on my neck. I tried to pull the collar of my blouse up to cover the bruises left behind by Frank's hand, but I knew it was no use. Even if I had been successful in hiding them, the healing gashes on my cheeks and forehead were still evident.

"Well, you're wrong. We're fine," I said defiantly.

He sat there for a moment and looked at me. I stared back, unable to take my eyes off of him. Something about the mixture of attractiveness, confidence, and kindness he exhibited made him very appealing and compelling. I just couldn't take my eyes off of him if I wanted to. He pulled his wallet from the back pocket of his jeans and laid three crisp twenty dollar bills on the table then stood from the booth.

I looked from the money to him and said, "What's this for?"

He shrugged. "For a rainy day."

"It's dry as a bone outside," I said and pushed the money across the table.

"I know. But you never know when it might start raining."

I folded my arms across my chest. "Look, I don't know what you think this money will get you, but I ain't no prostitute or crackhead."

His eyes changed. He actually looked a little hurt, but he didn't say anything. He simply shook his head and walked away, leaving the money behind. I watched as he reclaimed his seat at the counter. I sat there for a moment and the more I thought about the situation, the more upset I grew. Who was he to treat me like some kind of charity case? I grabbed Aaron's hand and the money and marched over to the counter. I threw the money onto his plate, right into a pool of ketchup.

"I said, I didn't need it!" I said angrily then walked out of the diner.

I was halfway down the sidewalk when I realized that I didn't pay for my meal. I turned on my heels to find myself face to face with Scott.

"I took care of it for you," he said.

I rolled my eyes. "Of what?"

"Your bill."

"I didn't ask you to," I said hostilely.

"I know. What is your deal? I'm only trying to help you!" he said raising his voice.

"My deal is that I don't need your help!" I turned to leave but stopped when I heard him say, "Where you're from, they don't say 'thank you'?"

I didn't bother to turn around. "I'm not thanking you for doing something I didn't ask you to do."

"Man, you're the meanest and prettiest girl I have ever met in my life."

I just stood there, taken aback by his words. The only thing floating around in my mind was that he'd said I was pretty.

"Can I at least give you and the little guy a ride somewhere?"

Those words broke down my defenses. The truth was that we had nowhere to go. We had no money and there was no way I could go back home. So I stood there and cried. And as the tears fell, Aaron looked up at me with those sad brown eyes. A few seconds later I felt Scott's hand on my shoulder.

"Please let me help you," he said.

And I did let him help me. He helped me get into a local shelter. He bought clothes and food for me and Aaron. He took me to church, and when it was time for him and his friends to return to Arkansas, he promised to come back and check on me. Almost three weeks later, he did just that. And when he left again, he took us home with him. Evidently, his parents had been taking people into their home for years. Aaron and I were just the latest in a string of people they'd helped. Scott was their only biological child, but they'd raised six other children as well—children of many races.

It wasn't long after I moved in with Scott and his parents that we became romantically involved and not long after that, we were married. The Grants welcomed me into their family with open arms.

As I walked through the building, smiling and waving at everyone as I headed to my office, I thanked God for sending Scott into my life and for saving me from the hell I'd once lived with Frank Freeman.

I quickly abandoned those thoughts as I passed Pastor Betty's office. I peeked in the door to find her seated at her desk, her head in her Bible as it was every morning. I softly rapped on the door facing and said "Good morning" in an upbeat voice.

She looked up at me and smiled, her eyes alert. "Good morning, sweetie. How's everyone on your side of town?"

"Well, Scott and the kids have gone fishing."

"Are the kids playing hooky from school, today?"

"No, ma'am. They're out for teachers' meetings or something like that. Well, I'll leave you to your Bible study. I'd better get to work."

"Meet me for lunch?" she asked.

I readily accepted her invitation despite the fact that I was pretty sure

Scott had told her about the past weekend—my meltdown with the kids. I smiled as I left her office and made my way down the hall to my own office.

I spent the morning returning phone calls and answering emails. Lunch with Betty was nice and she didn't let on that Scott had told her about the weekend. I think she was waiting for me to bring it up, but I didn't. I couldn't. I was actually beginning to feel normal again, and I knew bringing up my panic attack or my past or Frank would reverse that.

I was coasting along fine until I began to make my rounds through the shelters, starting with the women's shelter where several women and their children were housed for six-week intervals, at which time, the church helped them transition into an apartment. Most of the women were victims of domestic violence, but a fair share of them were also recovering drug addicts.

Upon my arrival, Bonnie, the onsite manager, insisted on showing me the new playroom. And that's when it happened. I walked into the room and saw the pretty doll house and the books and the toys and my mind instantly reverted to another place and time. In an instant, I was in a pink bedroom full of new toys and clothes and books. I was twelve-years-old again and I was in Frank's house. I could almost feel his breath on my neck and his hands on my body as I collapsed to the floor.

5

"WHERE I'VE BEEN"

I woke up and the smell of beef stew and mashed potatoes quickly told me that I was lying on a cot inside the shelter's first aid office—just around the corner from the cafeteria. As my eyes began to focus, I saw two pairs of identical green eyes staring back at me. Scott and his mother. I tried to sit up, but felt someone gently pushing me back onto the cot. It was Scott, no doubt. Wonderful, loving, understanding, Scott. Scott with the now hysterical wife.

"G? G, you alright?" He asked.

At that very moment, I realized that his being here meant I'd taken him away from his plans with the kids once again. I nodded and said, "I'm fine. You should get back to the kids…fishing."

"They're here. And it's okay. Fish weren't biting," he said in a reassuring voice as he brushed my hair from my face and kissed my forehead. I closed my eyes and tried to relax. I tried to soak up his love, because of everyone in the world, I knew that Scott loved me. I knew that without a doubt. He looked over at his mom and nodded and she gently patted my shoulder before leaving the small room and shutting the door behind her.

Scott leaned in close and said, "Now that we're alone, will you tell me how you really feel?"

I placed my hand on my forehead. "I'm...I'm fine, really."

Scott gripped my hand in his. "Please, G. Please tell me what's bothering you. *Please*."

I looked up at him, at the sadness and frustration in his eyes. And for the first time in a long time, I said the name aloud. "Frank...I saw him, in my mind."

"What did you see?"

I closed my eyes and tried to swallow, but my throat felt sticky and dry. I gulped and said, "The play room reminded me of my room at his house. It was beautiful and for two months, things were good." I stopped because I truly didn't want to go any further.

"G, please go on. Don't shut down this time. I want to know."

I struggled with the words as I fought to contain my tears. "Um, after the two months, he...he decided I was his woman and he..." That's when I broke down because those were words I'd never shared with anyone before. Scott held me tightly as he whispered words of comfort to me. He promised he'd be right there. He'd never leave me and he'd never let anyone hurt me again. I wanted to believe him, but nothing he said seemed to dent the deep sense of hopelessness that was buried inside of me.

Scott took me home long before the work day had ended and put me to bed that afternoon. I lay there listening to my children playing outside, to Scott banging pots and pans in the kitchen. I listened to the ringing phone and knocks at the front door. I listened as my children ascended the stairs and walked into their bedrooms at bedtime.

When Scott climbed into the bed next to me, I closed my eyes tightly and tried to mimic sleep. I don't know if he believed it, but he didn't bother me. He settled into his side of the bed and before long, I found myself actually drifting off to sleep, believing it was safe to do so. I was wrong. In my dreams, I was twelve again, in that room, with *him*…

I lay there in my canopy bed, eyes wide open. I'd been living there with Frank for a couple of months having admitted that I really had nowhere else to go. I didn't really know where my father was and my mother never told me where my grandmother moved to, so when Frank offered to let me live with him, I accepted. It helped that he told me he was abused by one of his mother's friends just as I'd been. He promised to take care of me and not to let anyone hurt me.

Those two months were good. He was kind to me, bought me furniture and clothes. Let me stay up as late as I wanted and didn't make me go to school. He even played video games with me. It was paradise to me. That night he was out on the road in his big rig, but I expected him back any day.

I was fast asleep when I felt someone sit down on the bed beside me. I froze and my breath caught in my throat. Who was it? Hadn't I locked the door before I went to bed? I felt a hand on my back and I let out a whimper.

"Little sister … little sister, it's me," Frank said. He always called me "little sister". He even told his friends I was his half-sister.

I released a relieved sigh and turned over in the bed to see Frank sitting there with a smile on his face. "Missed you, little sister. You been alright here by yourself? Not too scared?"

I shook my head. "I was okay."

"You have plenty to eat? Heaven check on you?" Heaven was his friend and a booster. Most of the clothes he bought me were from her.

I nodded.

Frank laid back on my pillow, his feet still on the floor. "Man, I'm tired. That was a long haul. I think I'ma try to find some local work. I hate to leave you here alone like this, but it ain't safe for a little girl on the road."

I nodded as I lay there looking at him. I was glad he was back.

"Did I wake you, little sister?"

"Yeah, but it's okay. I'm glad you made it back."

He grinned. "Aw now, couldn't leave my girl here all alone forever. I gotta take care of you."

I smiled and watched him close his eyes. Soon he'd drifted off to sleep right there next to me. A few minutes later, I was sound asleep myself. Or at least I was asleep until I felt a hand softly rest on my thigh.

"Little sister," Frank whispered. His mouth was so close to my ear that I could feel his breath. "Little sister," he said again. "You sleep?"

I opened my eyes and turned to face him. He smiled at me. "You sure are a pretty girl."

"Thank you," I said. But I felt my stomach twist into a knot. I almost felt nauseous. Something wasn't right.

"You like me?" he asked softly as he brushed a piece of my hair from my cheek.

My body went rigid. No...no...no...not Frank.

My alarm must have been evident to Frank. He brushed his finger against my cheek and said, "Hey, you don't think I'd hurt you, do you? Haven't I been good to you?"

I nodded.

"And ain't we friends?"

I nodded again.

"Look, I really care about you and I want to keep doing things for you, okay? I just need you to do something for me now. That's how it is with friends. Friends do stuff for each other."

"O...Okay," I said as I choked back tears.

And right there in my ivory-colored princess bed with the gold trim, on the pink and purple polka-dotted sheets, underneath my bright pink comforter, at the age of twelve, I became Frank Freeman's woman.

I didn't realize I was out of bed and on my feet until I heard Scott's voice which seemed to bring me out of a fog.

"G...G! What is it? What's wrong?"

Somehow I had stripped out my clothes and stood there naked and trembling. Scott's face read alarm and worry as he inched towards me. "G...G, it's me. It's Scott."

I shook my head because all I could see was Frank. I saw him everywhere—on the walls, in the window. The rational part of my brain told me this could not be, but I wasn't listening to it.

"G, let me help you, okay? It's me. It's Scott."

I backed away from him because Frank was clouding my vision. I knew it was Scott, my husband. I knew I loved him and he loved me, but there was a battle going on in my mind. I held my head in my hands and grabbed fistfuls of hair. I screamed, trying to quiet Frank's voice in my head. I backed into a wall and slid to the floor, still screaming. I banged the back of my head against the wall and screamed some more. From the corner of my eye, I could see a mess of curly hair framed by the doorway. Serenity.

I heard Scott saying something to her and then I watched him shut our bedroom door. When he sat on the floor beside me and pulled me to him, I didn't resist. It seemed that for the moment, my demons had left me alone.

6

"GOOD WOMAN DOWN"

I spent the next day in bed without regard to my job or my husband or my children. When I left Frank, broken and bloody on his bedroom floor, I vowed to never look back and up until now, I hadn't. I'd effectively blocked the years I was with him and replaced them with the years I was with Scott. But that phone call had triggered an avalanche of memories I was unable to stop.

As I lay there listening to the sounds of my home and my family, I could think of nothing but Frank and all the things he did to me. The *awful* things he did to me. He was haunting me—torturing me with memories and I hated him all the more for it.

I heard the bedroom door creak open and quickly shut my eyes. I wanted whoever it was to go away, *please*. But they didn't. I could feel their presence and hear their breathing. I heard soft footsteps and then I felt the lightest kiss on my cheek.

"Feel better, Mommy," Serenity whispered.

I felt a catch in my chest just over my heart and when she'd left and closed the door behind her, I clutched my chest and sobbed silently. I cried for my little girl who needed a mother. I also cried because I knew I was in no condition to be her mother.

Later that afternoon, the bedroom door opened again. It was Scott entering with a tray of food. I squeezed my eyes shut, but this time, I didn't fool him.

"I know you're not sleep," he said. "You need to eat, darlin'," he added in a gentle voice.

I didn't move a muscle. I just lay there choking back tears, wishing I could disappear.

Scott's voice broke as he spoke again, "Please, G. Don't shut me out. I just wanna help you."

The desperation in his voice forced me to move. I rolled over and faced him. He sat there on the side of the bed with tears in his eyes. I sat up and reached for him and we held each other for a long while. I felt horrible for what I'd been putting him through. He was a good man, but I knew that even he had his limits.

We finally released each other and I wiped his wet cheeks with my hand. "I'm sorry." I whispered as I rested my forehead against his. "I'm so sorry."

He kissed me softly. "I need you, G. The kids need you. "

I closed my eyes and traced his lips with my fingertip. "I know."

"I love you, G."

"I love you, too, Scotty."

He cupped my face in his hands. "Will you talk to my mom or maybe one of the counselors at the center?"

I shook my head vigorously. "N…no, I can't."

"Will you talk to me?"

I stared at him in silence.

"Please, G. *Please*, you've got to talk about this or else it's gonna keep popping up."

"It's never popped up before now," I said.

His eyes widened. "You don't remember do you?"

I frowned. "Remember what?"

He kept one hand on my face and placed the other over my hand. "When we were first married, you would wake up screaming almost every night. I would ask you what the nightmares were about and you always said you couldn't remember. It went on for a couple of months and then it just stopped. "

I sat and thought about what he'd said for a moment then said, "I...I don't remember. I'm sorry."

He shook his head. "It's ok, but you've got to face whatever happened to you."

I fell silent, trying to process what he'd told me. I thought I'd buried everything. How often were the memories really resurfacing?

"Please, G. I feel like I'm losing you. I can't do this alone."

I looked into his eyes. "Do what?"

"Help you. I can't help you unless you let me, unless you're willing to help yourself."

I closed my eyes and sighed. "Okay."

"Okay?"

"Okay, I'll talk to you. Just not tonight. I…I need time."

"Alright. How about the next time a memory comes, you tell me about it. If I'm asleep, wake me up. If I'm not with you, call me."

"Okay."

Then he fed me dinner and held me for the rest of the night. Throughout the night, I could feel his breath on my face as he softly prayed for me.

7

"IN THE MORNING"

I had a peaceful next few days, no unwanted visitors in my mind or my sleep. I almost felt human again—like a wife and mother. I went about my daily routine, relieved that I didn't have to hold up my end of the bargain with Scott. No dreams—no talking. I was fine with that because it had been my goal not to utter Frank Freeman's name or talk about the things I endured in his home with *anyone*.

In those days, I did tell Scott about some of my childhood, though— being raped by a friend of my mother's, being neglected and abused by my mother, herself. I talked about my sister, Mo, whom I loved dearly and still missed terribly. And I told him about my decision to run away at the age of twelve. All these things I'd told him in vague statements before. But this time, I told him details and watched as he fought tears. It wasn't hard to talk about life before Frank. Because life *with* Frank was so much worse.

I even told him about the phone call from my supposed sister. I showed him the phone number I'd saved on my cell phone and he promised to have the number checked out. That made me feel a little better. At least if the number checked out I wouldn't have to fear Frank's showing up.

I went back to work and apologized to anyone I even thought was privy of my actions at the women's shelter, but I avoided the playroom like the plague. There was no sense in doing anything that might conjure up those memories, those nightmares, again.

Work was fine, therapeutic actually. It kept my mind off of everything else. Other than Scott dropping by my office twice a day or Betty calling every other hour, everyone treated me as if nothing happened, and I was grateful for that.

***

I sat on the living room sofa with the kids watching some show on the Disney channel and listening to them chatter on about school. Shane and Serenity loved school, but Aaron mostly complained about the amount of homework he was being assigned—his usual fourteen-year-old angst. I listened attentively as Scott prepared to leave for work. Besides being a farmer, he was in charge of light and sound at the church and he produced the weekly radio broadcast. Once the church reached its goal of venturing into TV, Scott would produce that show as well.

I watched as he grabbed the snack I packed him then leaned over and kissed all three of the kids on the cheek. I could tell Aaron wanted to resist, but he didn't. Then Scott kissed me softly on the lips and said, "Be back soon. Love you."

"Love you, too," I said with a smile.

"Be back soon" always meant several hours. Scott would have to program the in-sanctuary screens with the scriptures his father requested and with the lyrics to that week's worship songs. Then he'd have to check the sound and recording equipment. Since he was such a perfectionist, I knew he'd be awhile.

After TV time, we all went to bed a little earlier than usual since we had church in the morning and I was just too tired to stay awake. It didn't take long for me to drift off to sleep as I wasn't in fear of having another dream. I went to sleep with thoughts of my husband and children in my mind.

And then, the dream began.

I was fourteen-years-old and I was in the bathroom when I heard his voice through the door.

"You alright, little sister?" Frank asked.

"Uh!" I grunted as I gripped the toilet bowl and braced myself as last night's dinner continued to come up. I'd been kneeling in from of that toilet vomiting for what felt like hours. My throat hurt and my head throbbed and I just wanted it to end.

"Sis, how long you been sick like this?"

In between heaves I managed to grunt out, "A...few...days."

The bathroom door swung open. "When was the last time you got your period?" he asked, urgency in his voice.

I gagged and shrugged. "I don't know?"

Frank grabbed my arm and pulled me to my feet. Spit and bile flew from my mouth as he gripped my chin and turned my face towards him. I groaned.

"Think, girl, think!" he said as his eyes locked with mine. "Has it been more than a month?"

I heaved and tried to think. I clutched my stomach and said, "I think so.

I think it's been two months since I had one."

Frank let me go and I collapsed in front of the toilet and began to dry heave. "Damn!" Frank yelled as he kicked the side of the bathtub. I stood up and washed my face in the sink.

"You think you pregnant?"

I dried my face, left the bathroom, and walked across the hall to Frank's bedroom. I lay down in his bed—the bed I'd shared with him for over a year. I closed my eyes and wondered how I was supposed to know if I was pregnant.

Frank stood in the bedroom doorway. "Do you?"

"I don't know," I said as I rolled over in the bed.

I was exhausted and hungry, but the thought of eating made me nauseous again. So I laid still and soon I'd drifted off to sleep. I don't know how long I'd been asleep when I heard Frank shout, "Get up!"

The anger in his voice rattled me to my core and I bolted upright in the bed. I'd never ever heard him sound like that before. I sat up on the side of the bed and watched as he tossed a small box onto the bed next to me. It was a pregnancy test. I picked it up and looked at him.

"Take it in the morning," he said.

"Okay," I said. "Can I lie back down? I don't feel so good."

"You got a bed," he said, coldly. Then he turned and left the room.

I stared after him. He was mad at me. Was it because he thought I was pregnant? If I was pregnant, was it my fault? Tears stung my eyes as I walked down the short hallway to the my bedroom and laid down in my bed, a bed I'd deserted shortly after I became Frank's woman. That's what I was, wasn't it? That's what he said. He said he loved me and that as long as our relationship remained a secret, he'd keep loving me. And I needed for him to love me. I needed for someone to love me. But now he was mad at me...

I sat up straight in the bed, breathing heaving breaths. I looked around my bedroom, my eyes finally settling on the digital clock that sat on the chest of drawers. It was after midnight and Scott's side of the bed was empty. *Good*, I thought. *Then I don't have to tell him about this.* I laid back in the bed and shut my eyes tightly as I prayed the dream was over, but I knew better.

Early the next morning after Frank bought the pregnancy test, I quietly tipped into the bathroom and read the directions on the box. Frank hadn't said a word to me since he put me out of his bed and I felt so sad. If being pregnant meant he was going to be mad at me, I sure hoped that the test was negative.

After I peed on the little stick, I sat on the toilet and closed my eyes. Please let it be negative...please let it be negative...

When I saw that it was positive, I slid to the floor in front of the toilet and cried.

"You pregnant, ain't you?"

I looked up to see Frank standing in the doorway. I hadn't heard him come in. I nodded as I wiped my wet face with my hands. Frank stood there and stared at me for what felt like hours. Then he sat down on the side of the tub and covered his face with his hands. He shook his head from side to side and then he began to cry. I reached over and touched his arm. He jumped.

"Don't touch me! I'm tryna think!" he shouted, his face still buried in his hands.

I shrank back and stared at him. Think about what?

We sat there in silence in the bathroom for a long while. I was afraid to move a muscle. Afraid of how Frank would react.

"Finally he said, "I'll call Heaven. She'll know someone."

"S...someone for what?" I asked cautiously.

"Someone to get rid of it."

8

"FADE AWAY"

I woke up weeping, clutching to Scott for dear life. He must've made it home just in time to witness my reaction to the dream. *Just in time.* He held me and rubbed his hand through my tangled hair and whispered loving, comforting words to me.

After my tears had ended, he asked me about the dreams and I told him about both of them. Then he said, "What happened to the baby, G?" He must've put two and two together and figured out that the baby would've been older than Aaron.

I shook my head and buried my face in his chest. "Scott…"

He lifted my face and kissed me softly. "Tell me, G."

I closed my eyes, released a ragged sigh, and began to tell him about one of the worst days of my life.

As it turned out, Heaven did know someone and a few days later, I was sitting in Frank's car staring out the window at the outside of a rundown apartment building somewhere in Memphis I'd never been before. Truthfully, in two years, I hadn't seen much more of Memphis than Frank's house, Heaven's house, and the library.

I nervously tapped my foot as I waited for Frank to return to the car. I stared at the rusty number eighteen that hung on the door of the apartment

I'd watched him enter. I stared at it, wondering who was inside and what they'd do to me or my baby.

My baby.

I rubbed my stomach as I continued to gaze at the door and finally, it opened. I watched as Frank emerged from the apartment, a serious look on his face as he pulled the collar of his leather jack up to cover part of his cheeks and ears and shoved his hands deep into his pockets. He quickly bounded down the steps, taking them two at a time. In the two years I'd lived with him, he'd gained some weight and his tall frame was now covered with a layer of fat, making him husky. He looked intimidating to say the least.

When he reached the car, he opened the door for me and said, "Come on."

Those two words were more than he'd spoken to me in over a week. It was good to hear his voice again and even better was the way his voice sounded. Not angry as before, but just a little nervous. Nervous I could deal with. His anger had been more than I could bear. I missed him and his love. He was all I had in the world.

I stepped out of the car and followed Frank up the paint-chipped white metal steps. When we reached the door to apartment eighteen, Frank placed his hands on my arms and then leaned over and kissed me softly on my lips.

"Everything's gon' be alright, sis. Just do what she tells you and everything will be okay," he said. He pulled me into his arms, enveloping my body. He held me tight and whispered in my ear, "Remember, I love you."

He let me go and knocked on the door. I stood next to him, my eyes locked on the door. Frank placed his hand gently at the small of my back and rubbed it reassuringly. After about a minute, the dingy door slowly creaked open to reveal a short, wide, caramel-skinned woman. Her light, light blond hair was fashioned in a greasy Jheri curl and fell just below her shoulders. She greeted us with a warm smile.

I walked into the dimly lit apartment which smelled strongly of turnip greens and some type of fried food. Pork chops, maybe. The living room we were standing in was small and cramped with rather ugly furniture. Except for the huge paintings of Jesus, JFK, and Elvis on the walls, it reminded me of home—my mother's home and that reminder made my stomach drop.

"Well, hello there, suga'. Ain't you a pretty little thing? What's your name?" she said as she rubbed my hair. I flinched and backed right into Frank who pushed me forward.

Before I could open my mouth to reply, Frank said, "Cleo."

The lady eyed Frank and said, "So this is your sister, Frankie?"

I was a little shocked at hearing this, but then I remembered that this was our cover story. I was his sister—not his lover.

"Yes, ma'am. Half sister," Frank said softly.

"Hmm, she don't look nothing like you. Must be yo' daddy's child. You know me and yo' mama was real close, God rest her sweet soul."

A strange look came across Frank's face. "Yes, ma'am. We got the same daddy."

She nodded. "Mmhmm. Well, Cleo, I'm Carlene. How old are you, baby?"

I looked at Frank, whose eyes were glued to something across the room. I looked back at Carlene and said, "Four...Fourteen, ma'am."

She frowned and glanced at Frank. "Lord, you girls is getting yourselves in trouble earlier and earlier. Well, come on in the kitchen. That's where we gon' do our business. Frankie, you can have a seat in here. It won't take us long."

Our business? I looked back at Frank as Carlene led me into the kitchen, my eyes pleading with him to come with me. He offered me a watered-down smile and mouthed, "I love you, sis." That offered little consolation to me as I entered the small kitchen where the food smell intensified. I had to fight back the urge to hurl all over the floor.

Her kitchen table was covered with four dusty place settings. It looked like those dishes sat on that table 24/7 without any thought of being used for anything more than decoration. She moved the dishes, sprayed some Lysol on the table, and wiped it with paper towels.

She handed me a cup of something brown and said, "Drink this up. Then take your pants and underwear off, suga', and lie down on the table."

I did as I was told. Whatever was in that cup tasted horrible and it burned my throat like fire. I gagged and frowned, but I drank it all up. After that, I took my pants and underwear off and climbed onto the table. I nearly jumped back up when I felt the cold, damp table against the skin of my behind, but instead, I eased myself down and rested my head against the hard surface. Carlene grabbed my hips with her huge hands and tugged on me until my bottom was at the edge of the table. I strained my neck, trying to see what was going on. My head was spinning and my vision was blurred.

"Lay back down and relax, suga'," she said.

I nodded and lay back down. I looked up at the ceiling and gazed at the brown water stains that seemed to form pictures and patterns. My eyes were growing heavier and heavier. All of a sudden, Carlene's face blocked my view of the stains.

"Let's pray, suga'," she said, her voice sounding hollow to me.

I nodded groggily. She took my hand in hers. Her hand felt cold and sweaty. "Dear Lord," she began. "Please guide my hands and bless me not to leave nothing behind in this child's body. Bless this baby that I'm about to take outta her to be an angel in your Holy courts. And finally, Lord, bless this child not to get no infection. Amen."

"Amen," I slurred in agreement.

Carlene's face disappeared from my sight, and the last thing I felt before I passed out was her putting something inside of me. The next thing I remembered was waking up in Frank's bed, Frank lying next to me with his arms wrapped around me.

Scott shook his head and said, "How could they do that to you? You were just a little girl."

"I thought I was, too. I thought I was just this skinny little girl, but after that day, I never felt like a little girl again."

The next morning at church, I was the first person at the altar. I kneeled down as the women of the church laid hands on me. I prayed for God to relieve me of the pain, the burden I'd been carrying for so long. And for two weeks, I had no more dreams.

9

"FLY AWAY"

When you're damaged, you never know when you'll have a bad day. For me, a bad day meant seeing Frank's face and remembering my life with him mostly in my dreams. Occasionally, I'd see something that reminded me of him or his house and memories would flood me while I was awake. But that hadn't happened since the playroom incident, thank goodness.

On this particular day, I was in the bathroom, on the toilet, staring at the linoleum on the floor when I remembered it.

I sat on the toilet, holding my head in my hands. I was pregnant again. I knew this to be a fact without the benefit of a pregnancy test because I felt the same as I had the other three times I was pregnant. And I knew it had been six weeks since my last period. After all, Frank had taught me to pay very close attention to my period.

I cried silently, not wanting to wake Frank up. The last thing I needed was for him to find out I was pregnant again. I couldn't deal with him putting me out of his bed again and ignoring me like he did every time I got pregnant. But more than that, I couldn't deal with another trip to Carlene's. I just couldn't. I didn't want to lie on her kitchen table again and smell greens or chicken or neck bones cooking. I didn't want to feel her insert things into my body. I didn't want to pass out from the hard liquor she gave me. I didn't want to hear another of her lectures on the importance of making sure my "boyfriend" used a condom when we had sex. And exactly what was I supposed to say to that? I couldn't tell her that the man she thought was my brother was really my boyfriend and that he didn't like to use condoms—or at least that's what he always told me.

I didn't want to bleed and hurt for days afterward or listen to her pray that my babies would be angels. I didn't want to watch as Frank paid her a bunch of money and then sat down on her couch and watched her TV like he did when he waited for me to get my hair fixed. I didn't want any of that stuff to happen, but I was pregnant and if Frank found out, that stuff was exactly what was going to happen.

I heard a knock at the bathroom door and quickly wiped my face. "Yeah," I said.

"You alright in there, little sister?" He jiggled the door knob. "Why you got the door locked?"

"I'm fine. I'm just finishing up." I flushed the empty toilet and ran some water in the sink for a few seconds. I opened the door and Frank eyed my suspiciously. "Um, I guess I locked it by accident," I added.

I tried to walk past him and he grabbed me around my waist and pulled me to him. He kissed my cheek and said, "You sure you okay?"

I avoided his eyes as I nodded. "Yeah, I'm fine."

He smiled. "Good, then come on back to bed. I was missing you."

I frowned. "Bed? Don't you have work?" Frank had sold his rig a couple years earlier and worked for a liquor distributor. He delivered liquor to several cities in Tennessee, but he never had to leave the state. He took the job so that he wouldn't have to leave me at home alone as he had in the past.

"Naw, I took off today."

My heart fell. I wasn't feeling well and I was looking forward to having the day alone to deal with my nausea. Now, I'd have to fight through the sickness if I didn't want Frank to know I was pregnant. And so, we went back to bed, where we spent most of the day. Doing what we always did— whatever pleased Frank and whatever my sixteen-year-old body could take.

That afternoon, I had to hold my breath as I cooked dinner for us. I loved cooking and I had tons of cookbooks to prove it, but the smell of that food made my head swim. I barely ate dinner and as I lay down in that bed next to Frank that night, I knew I wouldn't be able to keep him in the dark about the pregnancy for long.

By the time I was two months along, Frank still didn't seem to realize I was pregnant, but I knew I was running out of time and I'd have to figure something out and soon. So I decided to do what I knew best. I decided to run away. One night, while he was fast asleep, I stole a wad of money from Frank's wallet. I figured that that along with the allowance he'd given me to buy clothes from Heaven and to get my hair fixed at her cousin's house would be enough to hold me for a while. The next day I left him a note telling him I was leaving because I was pregnant and I didn't want to go back to Carlene's. Then I called a cab and thirty minutes later, I was headed to the bus station.

"G, you okay in there?" Scott's voice brought me back into the present.

I stared at the door, not sure for a moment that it was actually Scott's voice I'd heard.

"G?" he repeated.

"Y…yes, I'm fine. I'll be out in a minute." My hands shook as I moved to flush the toilet.

I stood at the sink and washed my hands. As I looked into the mirror, the reflection staring back was a sixteen-year-old version of me. I could see my boney frame accented with a growing belly. My unruly hair was pulled back into a ponytail. I was in the dingy motel room in Chattanooga, where I lived after fleeing Frank's home the first time.

The money I'd taken with me when I left Frank only lasted me a month and as I stood in that bathroom, I realized that my plan had failed. I was low on food and had basically been existing on hot dogs and water. I didn't know anyone and most of the men I met around that motel thought I was a prostitute. Sadly, that was probably the only way I was going to earn any more money. I was sixteen and pregnant and the only thing I knew how to do was cook and clean, and I quickly learned that no one was going to hire me to do even that without some ID and a social security card— neither of which I possessed. I didn't even have a copy of my birth certificate. So I was stuck right in between a rock and a hard place. I only had two options. I could call Frank and pray he'd take me back, or I could actually start taking those men up on their offers. I chose to take my chances with Frank.

I called him collect and when he answered, I told him where I was and asked him to come get me. He sounded relieved and a few hours later, he arrived at my room. He hugged me tightly and told me how much he'd missed me. He asked me if I was hungry and stopped by a McDonald's before we hit the highway. I was happy—no—ecstatic to be returning to the only real home I'd ever known.

Frank was quiet during the ride back home, but he'd reach over and grasp my hand and smile at me, like he really was glad to see me. The feeling was definitely mutual. I was more than glad to see him and I was thrilled that he wasn't mad at me for leaving.

By the time we made it home, I was close to peeing on myself, having held it for the entire non-stop trip. As soon as Frank unlocked the door, I rushed inside, making my way to the bathroom, but before I could get through the living room, and before Frank could shut the front door good, he grabbed me by the hair and pulled me to him. He twisted my hair in his hand, turning me to face him.

"Ow!" I shrieked. "Frank, you're hurting me!"

He brought his face close to mine and sprayed me with spit as he shouted, "What the hell is wrong with you?!" His voice was distorted with anger.

I shook my head and grabbed at his hand. He, in turn, gripped my hair even tighter. I grimaced. "Frank, please! It hurts!"

"Yeah, well, it hurt when my damn woman stole my money and took off. That hurt real bad!"

"Frank—"

"You need to apologize, sis. Running your little tail off like that. After all these years I been taking care of you!"

"I...I'm sorry, Frankie," I whined, tears wetting my cheeks.

But he didn't hear me. I didn't think it was possible, but he tightened his grip on my hair even more and led me down the hall to my room and flicked the light on.

"Look at this! Look at all these damn clothes and shoes and books. You get your hair done every week and you repay me by running off?! That's how much you appreciate me, sis?!"

"Frank, I'm...I'm s—"

He slapped and then he released his grip on my hair and shoved me, sending me to the floor. I skidded backwards on my butt and all of the pee I'd been holding rushed from between my legs forming a puddle on the hardwood floor.

"I'm sorry, Frank. I...I love you," I whimpered.

He pulled his belt from the loops of his pants in one swift motion and said, "I ain't never whooped you before because you always been a good girl. Always did what you was told. But tonight, I'ma whoop your tail. Get up!"

I shook my head and said, "Please don't."

"Get up!!!!" he screamed. I wondered if the neighbors could hear him. Would they help me?

"Please..."

He didn't wait for me to get to my feet. He began swinging the belt wildly, hitting whatever was exposed—my head, my arms, my chest. I pulled my knees to my chest and lowered my head. He continued to hit me on the back of my head...my shoulders. I could feel the welts forming. I cried loudly, begged him to stop, but he didn't until he'd worn himself out.

He was breathing heavily and sweating as he squatted beside me and said, "Tell me this, sis. You cheat on me while you was gone?"

I vigorously shook my head and sniffled. "N—n—no, I—I swear I didn't."

He stared at me. "You lying to me?"

My hand trembled as I raised it to wipe my face. I felt a welt that ran from just underneath my eye to my chin. It stung. "No. I didn't cheat on you."

He stood over me and gave me a skeptical look. "Well, you gonna have to prove it."

I rubbed the back of my sore head. "H...how?"

Frank smirked as he began to unzip his pants. "I think you know how."

Once Frank was satisfied I'd proven myself to him, he kicked me out of his room and his bed.

"You wanna have that damn baby of yours, then fine. Don't step foot back in my bedroom until you push that kid out. You ain't getting nothing from me but food and shelter. I'll teach you to leave me!" he said, and I knew he meant every word of it.

All at once, I was back in the bathroom of the home I shared with Scott and our children. The sounds around me were loud and confusing. Someone was screaming deafeningly, repeating the same word over and over again, *"No! No! No!"* Someone else was crying. Then I heard a rhythmic thudding sound and above the din of it all was Scott's voice screaming my name. I looked around the bathroom, trying to focus; trying to figure out was going on. It only took a second to realize that the screaming was coming from my own mouth. I was sitting on the bathroom floor, my vision blurred by a steady stream of blood. I reached up and felt a gash on the side of my head. One look at the sink told me that I must've fallen and hit my head on the way to the floor.

The thudding continued and I could tell it was coming from the door. I'd locked it and Scott was trying to break in.

"Scott," I said softly. "Scott, help me. Help me, please."

Finally the door burst open and Scott rushed in, revealing the source of the crying I'd heard. Standing just outside the bathroom door were all three of my children and Serenity was in tears.

10

"THE LIVING PROOF"

I lay in the hospital bed, staring out the small window at nothing in particular. Scott sat sleeping in a chair beside the bed. My eyes filled with tears as I looked at him. He looked disheveled as he slept. My problems were wearing on him and I felt like I was becoming more of a burden than a wife. I hated myself for what I was doing to my family. I hated myself for remembering.

I rolled over so that I faced the door and thought about seeing Serenity's wet face as she stood outside the bathroom door. I could see her face and Shane's, and Aaron's, and although Serenity was the only one of the three who was crying, it was the look on Aaron's face that upset me the most. It wasn't a look of pain or even pity, but a look of rage.

Was he angry with me, angry at my weakness? I know I was. I hated weakness. I'd prided myself on being able to press through the pain of my past and create a good life. I could've been a statistic, but I wasn't. Neither my mother nor Frank had broken me, or so I thought. But right at this moment, as I lay in a hospital bed with a concussion and bandages on my head, I seemed to be the textbook definition of broken.

"You awake?" Scott asked softly.

I turned over and nodded, then regretted the action as the room started to spin. I closed my eyes and said. "Yes. Have you been here all night?"

Scott stood and stretched. He ran his hand through his hair and said, "Yep, and all day. It's almost dinner time."

He reached over and caressed my cheek. I placed my hand over his. "You should go home and get some rest. I'll be fine," I said with a weak smile.

Scott shook his head. "No, I'm staying here with you for better or for worse."

I sighed. "Well, it can't get much worse than this."

He kissed my forehead. "Worse would be losing you. I still have you and I'm never letting go."

I looked into his eyes and saw his pain and my heart felt like it was breaking into a million pieces. "Maybe you should," I said softly.

Scott frowned slightly. "Maybe I should what?"

"Let me go. I'm only hurting you and the kids. Maybe we should just separate for a while."

Scott's frown deepened. "What? Why would you say something like that? Why would you even think that? No. No! We're not separating." He put his arms around me and squeezed my body tightly. "I'm not letting you go. We'll work through this. My parents can keep the kids a while if we need them to, but we're not separating." He paused to release me. Then he cupped my face in his hands. "No separating. You understand me. G?"

I nodded faintly, afraid to aggravate my injury. "Okay."

He kissed me softly on the lips and said, "Now that that's settled, I wanted to tell you about this idea I had."

"Tell me."

He sat down on the hospital bed beside me. "How about this: every time you have a dream or memory, I'll help you think of something good, a good memory, to counteract it."

I thought about what he said for a moment. "You really think that'll work?"

He nodded. "Yeah, I think it will keep the bad memories from overtaking you. You wanna try it?"

"I'll try anything."

Scott's plan seemed to work pretty well. As memories of Frank's abuse continued to surface, he would be right there with me, whispering words about the good times—the day he proposed, our wedding day, Shane's birth. His words always calmed me and reminded me of the blessings of my present life. Of course the memories were really milder ones—Frank throwing a beer bottle or can at me when I angered him, a slap or shove—nothing major. But I knew that there were other memories, ugly memories that were yet to surface. And I couldn't help but wonder if Scott's plan would be as effective with those.

***

The pains were so unbearable that I couldn't even muster up the strength to cry. I lay in the bed, moaning, knowing without a doubt that I had to be in labor. There was no other way to explain the excruciating pain I was feeling. Once it subsided, I looked at the clock. I'd read in a book that you needed to time the contractions. So far, mine were twenty minutes apart. I sat up in the bed, grateful that the contraction was over.

I rubbed my stomach as I stood and walked into the living room where I sat on the sofa and dialed the number to the mobile phone Frank had just bought himself—a Nokia something or other. It was really neat. He could take it anywhere and use it. He didn't answer the first call or the second or the third. By the time my contractions were only five minutes apart, I'd called him twenty-two times and he still hadn't answered.

I was beginning to panic. I was going to have this baby soon and I didn't want to have it alone. When I felt the gush of warm fluid escape from between my legs, I knew I was in trouble. Between contractions I tried to figure out what to do, who to call. 911? No, not 911. Heaven? Yes, I could call Heaven. And that's exactly what I did.

Heaven greeted me with, "You're pregnant?!" when I opened the front door to let her in. I nodded and then collapsed onto the sofa and groaned as another pain hit me. I curled myself up in a ball and squeezed my eyes shut. "Oh!!!!!" I screamed into the couch cushion.

"That dirty, low-down—I knew you wasn't his damn sister! I knew it! This is his baby, ain't it? I knew he was messing with you. I just knew it! That's why he ain't been letting me come around. He tried to pretend you'd left and gone to stay with your mama. Dirty, low-down—"

"Oh!!! Oh God!!!" I screamed. The pains were coming faster and faster—too fast for me to be concerned about what she was saying. Our secret was out, but at that point I couldn't have cared less.

"Did you call your doctor?" Heaven asked.

"Doctor? What doctor?" I managed to say.

Heaven raised her eyebrows and pursed her bright red lips. "Damn, you ain't got a doctor?"

I shook my head. "No—I—don't," I said as another pain hit me.

Heaven sighed heavily. She walked over to the phone and dialed a number. A few seconds later she said, "Hey, this is Heaven. I need you over at Frankie's house right now. Cleo's having a baby."

Heaven hung up and helped me to my bed. A few minutes later, she left me to answer a knock at the front door. When she returned, she had Carlene with her. I panicked. What was Carlene doing here? Another pain hit me as I struggled to my feet and backed against a wall.

"No, no, no," I mumbled. "S...stay away from me. Please stay away from me..." I began to cry as I slid to the floor.

"Suga'...suga', I'm here to help. Like I always do," Carlene said.

How was she going to help me? How had she ever helped me?

She walked towards me and I scooted into a corner. "Please...please I don't want no abortion," I said as I tried to breath.

She bent over and smiled at me. "Baby, it's too late for that. I'm here to help you deliver this baby." She reached for my hand. I shook my head and wiped my eyes and nose with a t-shirt that was lying on the floor.

Heaven stepped over to me. "She's a midwife, too, girl. Let her help you."

I looked from Heaven to Carlene. What choice did I have? I let Carlene and Heaven help me to my feet and then onto my bed where only thirty minutes later, I gave birth to a baby boy.

I woke up with a smile at the memory of giving birth to Aaron. I looked over at Scott whose eyes popped open when he felt me stir.

"You okay?" he asked.

I wrapped my arms around him and snuggled close. "I'm fine," I said as I allowed myself to drift back off to sleep.

Carlene stayed with us for several hours, telling and showing me how to take care of Aaron. I was glad she did, because otherwise, I wouldn't have had a clue what to do with him. After she and Heaven left, I went to my bed and laid Aaron next to me. When Frank finally made it home, Carlene instructed him to buy the baby a bed which he promised to do the next day. So, little Aaron would have to spend his first night in my arms. I fed him and soon we were both asleep. Later that night, I felt someone shaking me.

I opened my eyes and saw that Frank was standing over us. The room was dark making it impossible for me to see his facial expression, but I knew something was wrong. I just knew it.

"Get up," he whispered.

I eased out of the bed, leaving my tiny baby as I followed Frank down the hall to the living room. As soon as we sat on the couch he said, "Did you tell Heaven about us?"

I shook my head. "No."

"She said she knew. She was talking all crazy to me. How does she know?" he asked, wearing a look of desperation.

"I guess she just figured it out."

Frank stared at me for a moment, then said, "Figured it out? Naw, you told her, didn't you? You want me to get in trouble. You want me to go to jail so you can be with someone else."

"No, I don't," I said, but even as the words left my mouth, I knew he wasn't listening to me. There was no convincing him that I hadn't told our secret.

"Stop lying!" he shouted.

I stood from the couch and began to back out of the room. "I'm not lying, Frank," I said softly, hoping my voice would calm him.

It didn't.

Before I knew it, he'd sprung up from the couch and had his hand around my throat. That night, the same day our child was born, he beat me for hours. He punched me and kicked me and screamed at me. He beat me until I thought I would surely die. And then he raped me right there on the living room floor.

When I woke up the next morning, the first thing I heard was the distant cries of my baby. I needed to go to him. I needed to take care of him, but I couldn't move. Every inch of my body ached. My eyes were swollen shut, so I couldn't see. My nose throbbed and I could feel a trail of dried blood that ran from my left nostril to my top lip. I could only imagine how I looked.

Evidently I'd spent the night on the living room floor. I rolled from my back to my stomach and tried to lift myself up on my knees. I tried and I failed. After several more minutes of trying, I finally managed to get to my feet, but almost instantly fell onto the couch. My head ached and I felt so dizzy. I needed to get to my baby. I tried to stand again and I fell again. Then there was a knock at the door, a loud knock which seemed to intensify my headache.

"Who...who is it," I slurred.

"Cleo? Cleo, it's Heaven. Let me in. I came to check on you and the baby."

"Heaven? I...I can't get to my baby," I said as I began to cry, but it hurt to cry so I tried to stop.

"Cleo! Cleo, what's wrong? Open the door!" More knocking. "Cleo! Where's Frank?"

I gripped my aching head. "I don't know," I whimpered as I tried to pry my eyes open.

"Is he in there?"

"I don't know," I repeated.

Heaven jiggled the doorknob. "Cleo, can you open the door for me?"

"I can't see, Heaven. My eyes won't open."

"Oh, Lord. Try, Cleo. Try to open the door."

I struggled to my feet again and I fell again. So I crawled. I crawled to the door and after three tries, finally managed to feel the deadbolt lock and unlock it. I scooted away from the door and heard Heaven walk in. Then I heard her gasp. In an instant she was on the floor next to me.

She pulled me into a hug and said, "What did he do to you?!"

I cried and the tears stung as they seeped past my swollen eyelids. I cried and wailed.

"Shh," she said as she stroked my hair. Even that comforting gesture hurt me, and I flinched.

She held me like that for a long time. For as long as she thought I needed her to. Then she said, "I need to check on your baby."

I'd forgotten about the baby. He was still crying. I nodded and lay on the floor as she left to tend to my baby. I'd fallen asleep when she returned to the room. I had no idea how long I was out. "Here, put this on," she said as she dropped a sweat shirt, some underwear, a maxi pad, and a pair of jeans onto the floor beside me. It was then that I realized I was naked.

"And hurry up. We need to leave before he makes it back home. I guess he went to work," she added.

As bad as it hurt to move, I sat up on the floor and dressed myself as quickly as I could. Between my thighs was sticky with blood, but there was no time to worry about bathing and I knew it. Everything within me told me that if Frank came home and saw that Heaven had found me like this, he may very well have killed me.

Once we were in her car, headed to her house, Heaven talked non-stop. "I've been knowing Frankie for a long time, since we was kids. I always knew he was different, kinda weird. Always kept to himself mostly. Never saw him with no woman, either. When you popped up, I really wanted to believe you were his sister, but I couldn't. The whole thing just felt wrong—you living with him. I'd see the way he looked at you. I knew it. I knew it, Cleo, and I shoulda told somebody. Now look at you. I'm so sorry." Now she was crying.

I looked over at her through the one eye I had managed to open and shook my head. "It's okay," I said. But it wasn't okay. Nothing was okay.

"I'm calling the police when we get to my place. They need to lock his sick ass up!" She said as she slammed her hand against the steering wheel.

I shook my head. "No...no, don't. I don't wanna get him in trouble."

"Cleo, he damn near killed you! He needs to be locked up!"

I reached over and gripped her arm. "Heaven—no—please."

She turned and looked at me. "Why?"

"Because...because he's been good to me. Just...just don't call them. Please."

Heaven stopped her car in front of her small house and sighed. "Cleo, I want to help you, but I need to know the truth. "

I stared at the neat blue house and the tiny porch which was crowded with toys.

"Cleo, is that Frank's baby?"

I eyed her with my good eye and hesitantly nodded.

She leaned back in her seat. "He ain't your brother, is he?"

I turned and looked out the window.

"All those trips to Carlene's? Were those his babies, too?"

"Yes."

"Does he hit you a lot?"

I looked down at Aaron who was sleeping in my lap. "No. Not really."

"Not really?" she scoffed. "Cleo, you know you can't go back to him, right?"

"I know," I said quietly.

"Anybody you want me to call? Your family?"

"I don't have nobody else. Frank was all I had."

She turned her head and looked me in the eye. "Now you got me."

11

"REAL LOVE"

I woke up with my arms flailing. I was fighting someone or something—Frank? Scott reached for me, pinning my arms down at my sides. "G…G, it's me. Wake up. It was just a dream."

I tried to listen to him, but the sound of my own breathing in my ears was drowning him out, making it impossible for the calmness of his voice to sooth me, I squeezed my eyes shut and vigorously shook my head.

"G," he said softly. "Listen to me."

I grunted as I tried to snatch away from him.

"G, I need you to fight through it. Fight through it so you can hear me. We can beat this, but there's no victory without a fight. *Fight through it, G.*"

I felt myself begin to calm down a little and I stopped resisting his touch. Scott pulled me closer to him as he placed his lips on my ear and began to whisper.

"You know when I first knew I loved you?" he asked.

I gripped his arm and buried my face in his shirt as he continued to speak.

"It was those three weeks after I left you in that shelter in Oklahoma. I came back here but my mind was there, with you. You consumed my every thought. I dreamed about you and little Aaron—worried about y'all. All I could think about was how fragile you were. I remembered the bruises that were on your neck and how some monster had hurt you. All I wanted to do was to bring you back here so that I could protect you and take care of you," he said.

He tightened his grip on me and said, "When I made it back to Oklahoma and saw you and Aaron again, I felt so relieved and so happy. I knew right then that if you'd have me, I would make you my wife. It wasn't just something I wanted, it was something I needed. I *needed* to be with you forever. I knew I could never leave you again."

I smiled. "Even after the way I treated you when we first met? I was so mean to you."

"I'm a hunter, G. I love the chase," he said as he kissed me.

I patted his chest. "It's late and you've got work to do in the morning. I'm sorry."

"Don't worry about that. I hired a couple of guys to handle the stuff me and the kids usually do around the farm. There's nothing more important to me than you."

"And the kids," I said.

"Yes, and the kids. But I'm not worried about them and they're not worried about us. They're too busy at their Meme and Pawpaw's house swimming in the creek and jumping on the trampoline with their cousins."

"Well, I'm worried about them. Especially Aaron. He was young when we left Oklahoma and I don't know how much he really remembers about the things that happened back then. But you should've seen the look on his face when he saw me on the bathroom floor. It was downright scary. Reminded me of—"

Scott shook his head. "He's not him. He's nothing like him. He was just upset about seeing you like...like that."

I dropped my eyes. "So was I."

Scott lifted my chin with his hand. "Hey, we're gonna get through this, alright?"

"How do you know that?"

"Because I just do. Trust me."

If I ever trusted anyone, it was Scott. We lay back down in bed and I rested my head on his chest. We slept undisturbed until late the next morning.

***

The next morning, I awakened in bed alone. Scott left a note on his pillow letting me know that he had headed out to catch dinner. I knew he was in the woods, fishing at the little pond that he and the kids visited at least once a week.

I wrapped my robe around me and headed down to the kitchen where I planned to fix us both a light breakfast. I was in the middle of my second cup of coffee when I heard a knock at the back door. I headed to it with a smile and as I opened the door, I said, "Did you catch so many fish that you can't open the door?"

My smile quickly faded when I saw that it wasn't Scott at the door, but a man I'd never seen before.

He offered me a snaggle-toothed smile and said, "Um, excuse me, ma'am. I'm Lee. Um, is Mr. Grant in?"

"Lee?" I said, feeling a little wary of this stranger.

"Yes, ma'am. Mr. Grant hired me to help around here. Is he or Mrs. Grant here?"

I smiled slightly. I got that a lot. Scott was, for lack of a better word, the textbook definition of a redneck. He was tall and tan and well-built. He hunted and fished and drove a dusty pickup truck with a big razorback plastered in the rear window. He rode horses, raised cotton, and had a coop full of chickens in his backyard. No one would ever guess that he had an African American wife.

"*I'm* Mrs. Grant. My husband's gone fishing. Can I help you with something?"

His shock registered on his face loud and clear. "Oh, uh, well, I was just wondering about that old car over there." He pointed to an old Chevy that had been Scott's car in high school. "I was wondering if it was for sale."

I raised my eyebrows. "Oh, I don't think so." Just then I saw Scott emerge from the woods carrying what I was sure was a cooler full of fish in one hand and his fishing pole and a paper sack in the other. He smiled brightly as he approached us. He slid past me into the kitchen, set everything down, and wrapped his arm around my waist before turning to Lee.

"I see you've met Lee," Scott said. Then he pushed my hair back and kissed my forehead. "I see you've met my beautiful wife, Lee."

Lee stood there in stunned silence and I couldn't help but think that it was really silly for him to be reacting like that at this day and time.

Scott glanced at me and said, "You need something, Lee?"

"He wanted to ask about your old Chevy. I'll let you two talk," I said and ducked back into the kitchen. I was waiting at the kitchen table when Scott finally came in. "Well, Lee sure was taken with you," he said. "He could barely get a word out during our conversation."

I shook my head. "No, he was taken with you having a black wife."

Scott sat down across from me. "No, he was taken by the fact that I have a *beautiful* black wife."

I grinned. "Aren't you sweet…and idealistic? Anyway, what's in the sack?"

It was Scott's turn to grin. "A surprise for you—some Poke salad."

Now, that *was* a surprise. "Oh wow, fish and Poke salad! We are gonna eat good tonight! You are too good to me."

He stood and walked around the table. He crouched beside me. "I do have something else good in mind…if you're up to it, that is."

I leaned over and kissed him while silently thanking God that my memories of Frank had never spoiled my intimacy with Scott. I prayed that that would never change. I prayed that at least that one part of me would still belong to Scott. As he took me into his arms and began to give his love to me, I was relieved that not one thought of Frank Freeman or his abuse entered my mind.

12

"YOU REMIND ME"

Sunday as a Grant always meant church, church, and more church. From the early-morning prayer gathering to the 6:00 P. M. evening service, Sunday was a day designated exclusively for worship and I loved it. I absolutely loved listening to the choir sing and to my father-in-law preach. I loved the feeling of being involved in corporate worship and praise. I loved being in the presence of God.

I was particularly excited about church this Sunday, because I would get to see my kids for the first time since they'd begun staying with my in-laws. It had been more than a week since I'd looked into Serenity's green eyes or ran my hand across her mass of hair. I missed hearing Shane's squeaky voice and seeing his gap-toothed smile. And I missed seeing the dimple in Aaron's right cheek when he smiled and hearing him call me "Ma" in a voice that seemed too deep for my little boy.

We arrived early, as usual, and were met by our children as they bounded out of the church doors and nearly knocked us down with hugs and kisses. I wanted to cry tears of joy, but I didn't. I was afraid they'd misinterpret them as tears of sadness. So I smiled and hugged all three of them and kissed their foreheads and cheeks.

Serenity never left my side all day. And Shane stayed glued to his father. After a warm greeting, Aaron was pretty standoffish. Scott tried to convince me that it was just his age. That maybe Aaron thought it was childish to hang under your parents. I wasn't buying it, and I decided that as soon as I could get Aaron alone, I was going to talk to him and make sure he was okay.

The opportunity presented itself when we were at my in-laws' house for dinner. Everyone always met up at their cabin for Sunday dinner and then we all headed back to the church for evening service. Around the table sat Rev. and Mrs. Grant as well as Scott and me and the kids, Scott's six siblings, and their families. Well actually, the adults crowded around the table and the kids ate in the den and even outside on the deck.

After dessert, I found Aaron sitting alone on a tree trunk at the edge of the woods that surrounded the Grant home. I walked over to him, sat down, and smiled at him. He returned my smile and then his eyes quickly darted from me to the kids playing on the trampoline to the right of us.

"I miss having you guys at home. But that'll change soon," I said softly.

Aaron shrugged. "It's okay. I like being here. At least I don't have to just hang out with Shane and Serenity. I got my cousins and stuff."

I nodded. "Well, I'm glad."

We were both quiet for a few moments and then I said, "Are you okay, Aaron?"

He gave me a confused look. "Yes, ma'am?" he said as if he wasn't sure if his answer was correct.

"Good, because I worry about you."

"You shouldn't. I'm fine," he said, but I could tell he was just trying to ease my mind.

We sat there quietly for a few moments and I had just about decided to leave him alone when he said, "I remember some stuff about him."

"About who?" I asked as if there was any question who he was talking about.

"*Him.* My…my father. My real father. I remember him being real mean to you."

"Yes, he was," I said softly.

"I remember him yelling and throwing stuff at you, and…" He stopped and looked down at the trampled leaves under his feet.

I placed my hand on his arm. "What, Aaron? What is it?"

He looked up at me with a look of sadness on his face that was heartbreaking. "I remember you being on the floor and he…he was kicking you." He clenched his fists and quickly stood to his feet, shaking his head.

I was shocked. Aaron was only three when that happened. It was the last beating I would endure before I finally left Frank. I stood next to him and wrapped my arms around his stiff body. It was only a few seconds before he relaxed his posture and hugged me back. He laid his head on my shoulder and sighed. But he didn't cry. I think to him, crying would've been a sign of extreme weakness. And Aaron abhorred weakness as much as I did.

I released him and cupped his face in my hands. "I'm so sorry you witnessed that and I'm sorry it's still in your memory. But he can't hurt me now."

Aaron nodded before hugging me again and then leaving me. He walked over to the crowded trampoline with his siblings and cousins. I sat back down on the log and thanked God that Aaron didn't remember what Frank did to him.

***

It had been two weeks since my last dream or memory and I finally convinced Scott that it was alright for the kids to come home and for me to go back to work. My first few days at work were pretty routine—meetings, counseling sessions, phone calls, emails, and so on. It felt good to be back and to take my mind off of my problems and focus on helping others. Scott met me for lunch every day, and I knew that was just his way of checking on me. I didn't mind. Nothing eased me like seeing his smiling face. I'd never be able to thank God enough for him.

It was on a Thursday afternoon that I first saw him. He was tall and thin with chocolate brown skin. He walked with a limp and his clothes looked a little worn. When I asked Betty about the new janitor, she said his name was Rodney and that she'd hired him while I was off. He replaced Carl who'd worked for the church for years before he fell ill.

I couldn't put my finger on it, but something just didn't set right with me about him. It was the way he looked at me, as if he knew me. I'd never met this man before. I would've remembered if I had. But still, there was a familiarity about him that made me very uncomfortable.

So I was upset with myself when I realized that I had become so engrossed in my work that by the time I was ready to leave, I was the only person left in the building. Me and Rodney, that is. I met him in the hallway and that is when I realized why he was so familiar to me.

As I closed my office door and began walking towards the exit, I passed right by him and said, "Good evening."

"Good evening, little sister," he replied and the blood drained from my face. The next thing I knew, I had dropped my purse on the floor and was running towards the exit. My hands shook as I unlocked my car door. I was in my car when I saw him coming towards me with my purse in his hand. I started my car and my tires squealed as I raced from parking lot, leaving Frank Freeman in my dust.

14

"MIDNIGHT DRIVE"

I roared into my driveway, sending loose gravel and dirt flying into the air. Before I could climb out of my car, Scott came running from the house towards the car, a look of alarm on his face. I rushed to him and collapsed in his arms.

"G, what's going on? My mom called and said that Rodney called her. He said you ran out of the building like something was chasing you. Said you left your purse behind."

I nodded vigorously. "It was him. I had to get away."

Scott released me and gave me a look of confusion. "Get away from who? Rodney?"

"Yes. He's Frank! He called me 'little sister' and his face...I know it's him."

"Okay, calm down, G. Let's go inside so that you can tell me what happened."

I followed him into the kitchen where I noticed how empty and quiet the house was. "Where are the kids?" I asked.

We both sat down at the table. "Upstairs. Now, tell me what's going on." Scott said.

"I knew something wasn't right about him and then when he called me' little sister', I knew why. It's him!"

"Wait, he called you 'little sister'? When?"

"When I was leaving, I said, 'good evening' and he said, 'good evening, little sister .'"

"G, maybe he meant 'little sister' like in a Christian way. We call each other brother and sister all the time at church."

I shook my head. "No, it was the *way* he said it. I know it was him!"

"What do you want to do?"

"Call the sheriff so they can arrest him!"

He reached across the table and clutched my hand. "Arrest him for what, G?"

"For child molestation and rape and assault!" I nearly screamed.

"G, you can't prove any of that. It would be his word against yours," he said, giving me a look of pity.

"*This* is the proof!" I yelled as I stood, pulled my shirt up, turned around, and showed him the scars on my back left behind by Frank's belt. "And this!" I pointed to the small hump in my nose, evidence of it having been broken. "You need more proof?!"

The chair screeched against the wood floor as Scott stood and cautiously walked towards me. "G—" he began.

"And Aaron—Aaron is proof! I was only sixteen-years-old when I had him. Frank was at least thirty!"

Scott reached for my arm and I snatched away. "G, I understand. I'm on your side," he said.

I glared at him. "No, if you were on my side, you wouldn't be shooting down every word that comes out of my mouth! You don't believe me, do you?!"

Shane appeared in the doorway to the kitchen. "Shane, back upstairs, bud," Scott said.

Shane disappeared without a word. "G, you gotta calm down. Let's just sit down and talk about this."

"Talk? You don't wanna talk, Scott. You don't believe me. You don't believe it's him." I snatched my keys up from the table and stalked towards the front door.

"G!" He shouted as he ran behind me. "G! Stop!"

Turning a deaf ear to him, I quickly climbed into my car and began to back onto the rural road. As I drove away, I could see Scott in the rearview mirror, standing in front of the house with his hands on his head, screaming my name.

***

I drove around for hours, racing up and down rural roads, travelling to neighboring counties, before finally ending up right back in West Memphis. I checked into a roadside motel and collapsed into bed. I was asleep in seconds.

My dreams were full of distorted images of Frank chasing me through the woods that surround my home—Frank beating me—Frank beating my children—Frank laughing at me—Frank, Frank, Frank. Maybe "nightmares" is a better word for what invaded my mind all night long. Nightmares, terrors, you name it. One thing was for certain, I had to rid my mind and my life of Frank Freeman for good.

I sat up on the side of the lumpy motel bed and stared at the window. Light peeked in around the thick curtains alerting me that the sun was up and that I had been away from my family for an entire night—and I missed them. I owed Scott an apology. How could I expect him to understand how it felt to see that man and hear him call me by a name that sent shockwaves through my body? How could he understand what I had never bothered to fully disclose to him? Frank had abused and terrorized me on a level that I couldn't even explain. I feared him, but more than that, I hated him. Only *I* understood that and only *I* could deal with it.

I stepped into the cramped bathroom and washed my face with a dingy towel, rinsed my mouth out with water, and ran my fingers through my hair. I grabbed my keys and as I opened the door, the bright sunlight blinded me for a moment. It took a minute for him to come into focus. Standing in front of his truck was my husband, leaning against the grill with his arms folded across his chest. And seeing the deep concern in his eyes, brought tears to mine.

"I'm sorry," I said softly.

"So am I," he replied.

We stood there and stared at each other for a few moments before he slowly began to make his way to me. He reached for me and I welcomed his embrace.

He rubbed my back and said, "I love you, G. Please don't run away from me again. I love you so much."

"I love you, too. And I won't run away again. I promise." I meant every word. I wouldn't run from the one person I knew truly loved me again.

But, as I stood there in his arms, I made another promise—a silent promise. I promised myself that I would not stop until I proved that man was Frank. And if it took me until my dying day, I was going to make sure he paid for what he did to me.

My first course of action was to begin to live my life as normally as I could and to convince everyone that I no longer believed the janitor was my ex-tormentor and the father of my oldest child. It was a hard task, because the man stayed on my mind. But I managed by avoiding him for the most part. I made sure to keep my office door locked when I was working and I left with everyone else—no more working after hours. I was just biding my time, though. Waiting for a window of opportunity. I knew that if I was patient, a day would come when I could get the information I needed.

In the meantime, dreams and images continued to haunt me, though not as frequently as before. And of course, Scott was right there with me, whispering sweet memories into my ear. Reassuring me that everything would be okay, and covering me with his love. I spent more time with my kids, hoping to undo the damage I had already caused with my erratic behavior. One thing no one can doubt is that I love them and all I do is to protect them.

I had to get the goods on this man and stop him for good. And my husband had a cabinet full of guns to aid me in my mission. But first things first. I needed proof of who he was, and that would take time. Yes, I'd have to be patient. But that was no problem. I could be very patient when I needed to.

15

"SEARCHING"

I was busy working when I heard the conversation outside my closed office door. I can't be accused of eavesdropping since I had my door closed and Arthura and Tammy (two of the counselors) decided to hold a conversation in the middle of the hallway, just outside my door.

"Well, there's mess in the cafeteria. One of our residents got sick and lost her lunch all over the floor. And guess who they expect to clean it up?" Arthura sounded frustrated.

"Not you!" Tammy said, sounding overly appalled. "Where's the janitor? What are they paying him for?"

"Apparently, he's sick. Called off work early this morning. Oh, well, I might as well get to it."

"I'll help."

As they trotted down the hall, a smile spread across my face. This was my chance. I called Scott and told him I'd be working late.

I waited patiently for the building to empty. I sat at my desk until the place was so quiet you could hear a pin drop. Then I walked quietly through the building, checking every nook and cranny to be sure it was empty. Next, I headed for the janitor's closet where, to my disappointment, I found nothing more than cleaning supplies. I was hoping he'd have something in there of a personal nature, but he didn't.

My next stop was my mother-in-law's office. I needed to get in there and look through her personnel files. The problem was that I had no idea where she kept them. She was a wonderful, sweet woman, but her organizational skills left much to be desired. I spent way too long rifling through piles of paper and searching cabinet drawers before finally finding what I was looking for.

Rodney Kemp lived in an apartment complex in the middle of town. His driver's license said that he was forty-five years old which put him right around Frank's age. As I stared at the photocopied driver's license photo, I tried to find something that reminded me of Frank, but I couldn't. Then again, it had been several years since I'd left him behind. And the beating I'd given him probably had altered his looks at least a little.

I quickly jotted down his address and replaced the file before slipping out of the office, down the hall, and out to my car. I drove by the apartment complex on my way home. Well, actually, I parked in the parking lot and stared at the illuminated window that was next to the front door of apartment six. I wondered who was inside with him. Was it another young girl? Was he ruining her life, too?

Those thoughts made me want to bolt from that car and break the door in. But I knew I had to stay calm. If there was a girl in there, busting in there wouldn't help her. It would only make me appear crazier than everyone already thought I was. I closed my eyes and said a silent prayer for his possible victim before making my way home to my family.

After a late dinner, I climbed into bed with my husband and held him close as I drifted off to sleep.

***

It had been two months since Heaven found me, since she saved me. She was a good friend in every way. She gave me shelter, nursed me back to health, and helped me with Aaron. I owed her a debt that I would probably never be able to repay. I was eternally grateful to her.

In two months' time, Heaven, who seemed to have unlimited connections, managed to get me a fake ID and social security card. She helped me apply for public benefits, so I could buy diapers and formula for the baby. I couldn't give her much money, but at least my food stamps contributed some to her household. I did all of the cooking and Heaven and her kids seemed to appreciate it. I tried to keep the house clean and I babysat her daughter, Sasha, and her son, Fernando, whenever she needed me to. She even promised to show me how to "lift" as she termed it. I wasn't all that excited about learning how to steal, but I was willing to learn whatever my friend wanted to teach me.

Not a day passed when Frank didn't call looking for me. Heaven always told him she didn't know where I was. But he knew better. He even came by her house a couple of times, but Heaven's threats to call the police and tell everything sent him away quickly.

I felt safe in Heaven's little house, with her family. I missed Frank in a way, because for four years, he was truly the only family I'd known. He was all I had, but I knew there was no sense in dwelling on that. I couldn't go back to him. My first beating had been punishment for leaving him. The second came because he believed I'd told his secret. Now, I'd left him again and I was living with the one person to whom I actually had revealed our secret. My punishment would be beyond brutal if I returned to him. No, I couldn't go back.

I squeezed my eyes shut and pulled Aaron close to my bosom. What would Frank do to him if he had the chance? Though I'd heard him scream through Heaven's door about seeing the baby, I knew that was just a ploy. He'd never wanted a baby. The many trips to Carlene's bore the proof of that. Would he hurt Aaron? The thought scared me more than facing another beating from him. I kissed Aaron's forehead and whispered, "I won't let anything happen to you."

***

I was sitting in Heaven's living room watching TV when I heard a knock at the front door. I didn't move from my seat on the couch. I never answered her door when she wasn't home—just in case it was Frank. And besides, Heaven didn't tell me to expect anyone. So I sat there and held my chubby four-month-old baby in my lap and kept my eyes glued to the TV. When I heard keys rattling, I thought that maybe it was Heaven. Maybe she'd knocked because her hands were full. I laid Aaron on the sofa and went to open the door for her. But the door flung open before I could reach it.

Instead of Heaven, Ernesto stepped inside. I knew he was the father of her kids, but she never told me he had a key to her house. Panic deluged me. Ernesto was Frank's friend. Up until that point, Frank only thought I was staying with Heaven. Now Ernesto would be able to confirm his suspicions.

We both stood frozen by a mutual sense of shock. "Cleo? Whachu doing here?" he said, his eyes shifting from me to Aaron. "Frankie's been tryna find you! I can't believe Heaven's had you here the whole time."

"Please don't tell him where I am," I said, my voice trembling. Tears were teetering at the edges of my eyelids. My mind was racing. I was going to have to find somewhere else to go and soon.

"Why are you hiding from him? He's really worried about you. He's outta his head."

He'd have to be out of his head to beat me like he did, I thought. "He...he hurt me."

"What? Come on. He's your brother and he cares about you. Heaven's been feeding you a bunch of lies. You can't believe her."

I ignored his statement. "What...what are you doing here?"

"My kids live here."

"They're at school."

"Yeah, well, I was gonna wait for them. Be here when they get home. I'll just come back."

"Please don't tell Frank you saw me. Please."

As Ernesto walked out the door, he simply shook his head in silence. And I knew he was headed straight to Frank, to tell him what I'd begged him not to. No sooner than he shut the door behind him, I jumped up from the sofa and headed to Sasha's room. I laid Aaron on the bed as I haphazardly shoved mine and Aaron's few clothes into one of Heaven's duffel bags. I quickly scrawled Heaven a note and called a cab. I had my welfare money and the money I'd made from shoplifting. That would hold us for a little while.

As I waited for the cab, which seemed to take forever making it to the house, I had no idea where I was going. It didn't matter. I just had to get away from there. Because Frank was coming; I knew he was.

After what felt like an excruciatingly long time, I heard the cab pull into the driveway. I didn't wait for the driver to come to the door. I grabbed the duffel bag and swung Aaron on my hip all the while heading to the door. When I opened it, my heart jumped into my throat. It wasn't the cab, it was Frank.

Frank looked just as shocked to see me as I was to see him. As he ascended the front steps, my instincts kicked in and I slammed and locked the door. I dropped the duffel bag and readjusted Aaron on my hip as I ran to the back door and made sure it was locked. I could hear Frank pounding on the front door, screaming, "Sis! Sis, open the door!"

My panicked movements had frightened Aaron and he wailed loudly as I hurried into Sasha's bedroom and sat on her bed. I wanted to cry but no tears came. Maybe I was just too scared to cry.

Boom! Boom! Boom!

The sound was so loud; he had to be kicking the door now. Aaron was crying uncontrollably, undoubtedly feeding off of my fear. I clutched him tightly and tried to whisper reassuring words in his ear, but it did no good. Still there were no tears from me. I considered calling the police, but even in my fear, my first instinct was to protect Frank. I still didn't want to get him in trouble. But if he didn't stop, I was sure Heaven's neighbors would call the authorities.

As soon as that thought ran through my head, the banging stopped. The only sound in the house was Aaron's cries. Everything else was eerily quiet. Had Frank managed to break the door down? Was he on his way to this room, to me, right now? I rocked Aaron back and forth and at the same time realized I needed to pee badly. My weak bladder had always been a problem for me. It was one of the reasons my mother abused me. I'd wet the bed up until I was nine or ten. And right then, I knew I was about to wet Sasha's bed. But I was too scared to move.

After several minutes of silence, I decided that maybe Frank was gone. Maybe a neighbor saw him and shooed him away. But that was unlikely. If he was inside the house, surely he would've found me by now. So where was he?

My answer was more knocking, but this time it came from the back door.

Bang! Bang! Bang!

Startled, I sprung to my feet. Why, I don't know. Where could I go? Out the front door? There was no way I could outrun him with Aaron on my hip.

Bang! Bang! Bang! "Cleo! Open the door!!"

Aaron, who had almost quieted during the break in the knocking, began to cry again.

Bang! Bang! Bang! "Little sister, please!"

I stood frozen. Aaron continued to cry.

Bang! Bang! Bang! "Little sister!" Frank's voice sounded unsteady. Like...like he was crying. Was he really crying?

I laid Aaron down on Sasha's bed and placed a pacifier in his mouth. He promptly spit it out and resumed crying. I patted his back. "Shh," I said. "Don't cry. Mommy will be right back."

My words seemed to provide no comfort for my small son. He continued to cry as I inched my way down the hall towards the kitchen. By the time I reached the back door, the banging had stopped. I cautiously slid the yellow curtain to the side and peered out the window that made up the top half of the door. With all of his banging, it's a wonder Frank didn't break the window.

The sight on the other side of the door shocked and confused me. Frank was sitting on the bottom step, his head in his hands, his body shaking. I could hear him crying through the door. And for some reason, now the tears came. The tears came because I felt sorry for Frank. I stared at him as I cried for him.

He sat there like that for a long time. I could hear him repeating the words, "I'm so sorry. I'm so sorry..."

And I believed that he really was sorry. I believed his tears were real and after I wiped the tears from my face, I unlocked and slowly opened the door. Frank's head snapped up and at first he just sat there like he wasn't sure he really heard the door open. Then he stood and turned around, his eyes swollen and red, his face streaked with tears. His chin and cheeks were covered in ragged stubble. His clothes hung from him—he'd lost weight in my absence.

"Little sister?" he said as if he was uncertain it was really me he was looking at.

"Frank..." I said and then broke down in tears again. Frank rushed up the steps, his arms outstretched. I scrambled backwards, afraid I'd made a mistake. Afraid he was going to hit me.

"Little sister, come here," he said softly. I didn't move. He stood in the doorway, a pained look on his face.

I shook my head. "You...you hurt me," I said. Those words were the only thing in my mind.

He leaned against the door facing. "I know. I'm sorry."

"You...you broke my nose."

A startled look crossed his face. "I...I did?" Tears streamed down his face. "I'm sorry. I'm so sorry."

"My eyes were so swollen I could barely see for weeks. You hurt me."

Frank folded his arms around his own body and slid to the floor.

"I know...I know. Please forgive me. Please."

I stood there and watched him cry some more and I started to think that maybe I shouldn't have left him. He seemed so upset, defeated really. He'd really missed me.

After several minutes, he wiped his face with the sleeve of his shirt and looked up at me. "Can I see the baby?"

The baby. Frank's breakdown had caused me to forget about my son, our son. I left Frank in the kitchen, made a quick stop in the bathroom, and walked into Sasha's room to find Aaron fast asleep. He must've cried himself to sleep. I lifted him from the bed and took him to the kitchen. Frank stood and walked over to me. He took Aaron into his arms and kissed forehead.

"He's a big boy, now," he said.

I nodded.

We stood there like that for a while, Frank holding Aaron, me watching them. And for a brief moment, it felt like we were a real family—mommy and daddy and baby.

Frank kept his eyes on Aaron as he said, "Come back home."

"I can't," I said softly.

"I promise not to ever lay another hand on you. I promise. I was just scared. Scared Heaven or Carlene were gonna tell about us and I'd lose you. I just didn't want you to get sent back to your mama. You're still a minor, remember?"

He was just trying to protect me? That thought had never

occurred to me.

"I need you, little sister. I'm don't know what to do without you. I...I want us to be a family, you and me and the baby."

I fumbled with the hem of the t-shirt I was wearing and fixed my eyes on the tiled kitchen floor. "But everyone thinks I'm your sister."

"I know. I was thinking we could move. Start over somewhere else. That way we don't have to lie about what we really are," he said. He leaned in and kissed my cheek.

I stared at him for a few moments. I wanted to believe him. I needed to believe him. Maybe what we'd had all those years was worth another try.

I reached for Aaron. "Let me get him ready. And I need to leave Heaven a note."

Frank wore a relieved smile when I turned to leave the kitchen. Thirty minutes later, we left Heaven's house. Two weeks later, we left Memphis. I never saw my friend, Heaven, again.

16

"HURT AGAIN"

I woke up in bed alone, my head pounding from frustration. I sat up and stared out the window at the full moon as I tried to calm my throbbing heart. The dream had been so vivid, so real. I wished I could go back to that day knowing what I know now. I wished I could tell my sixteen-year-old self to run in the opposite direction of Frank. But I doubt I would've listened. I loved him—or at least I thought I did. How could a person love someone so abusive? Even our "relationship" was a form of abuse. I was a child and I was his lover. There was nothing right about any facet of my relationship with him, but at the time, I didn't know that.

I swung my feet around and stood from the bed. I walked through my old house, looking for Scott. The only sound heard was the creaking of the floorboards beneath my feet as I walked from room to room. I checked the kids' rooms, the bathrooms, and the kitchen. I finally found him in the living room, kneeling in front of the couch. His eyes were closed, his hands clasped in front of him. He was praying.

I quietly walked over to him, kneeled beside him, and rested my hand on his back. He opened his eyes, looked at me, and smiled. He took my hand in his and we prayed together. When we were finished, we went back to bed and held each other all night long. I didn't bother to tell him about my dream, but he knew I'd had one. That's why he was praying. That night and in those moments, I knew more than ever how fortunate I was to have Scott in my life. I fell asleep thanking God for him.

***

Of all the places we'd lived over the years, I liked Tulsa the least. The duplex we lived in was small and cramped and the dark wood-paneled walls made the place seem downright claustrophobic. And it reminded me of the horrible little duplex I ran away from—my mother's home. I was reminded of her and how much I despised her. But it also reminded me of how much I missed my sister, and that was more agonizing than anything. By then I was nineteen. That would've made Mo twenty-three. I was sure she was long gone—far away from Arkansas. I rested my back on the sofa and thought about how great her life was probably going.

The day all hell broke loose, I was sitting on the sofa watching my three-year-old son as he sat on the floor playing with his toy truck. Life was ok for us. Frank had only hit me three times in the past three years. And usually I did something to upset him. Like the time I didn't have dinner ready when he made it home from work. That was totally my fault. I'd been next door chatting with Ms. Sevier, who was our neighbor and our landlord.

She'd invited me over for cookies and coffee, and although I didn't particularly like coffee, I did like her company. I let the time get away from me and by the time Frank made it home, I was only half-finished making dinner. He was tired from working his factory job and he'd slapped me pretty hard. But then he'd quickly apologized. I made sure dinner was on the table waiting for him when he made it home from then on.

I'd been taking birth control, so I hadn't gotten pregnant again. That was one problem we didn't have to worry about, or at least that's how Frank put it. "One kid is more than enough," he said. I liked being a mother and wanted a bunch of kids, but I would never go against Frank's wishes. I knew the consequences of doing that.

The knock at the door startled me. It was loud and really more of a bang than a knock. I knew it wasn't Ms. Sevier because she was too weak to knock that loudly. I opened the door to find her grandson, Seth, standing on the other side, smiling brightly.

"My grams wanted me to come change the filter in the heating unit," he said. Seth was a college student and in his spare time, he worked for his grandmother as a handy man. Ms. Sevier owned property all over Tulsa, so she kept Seth pretty busy.

I smiled and said, "Okay." I let him into the duplex and watched his every move. He was tall and well-built. His skin and hair were dark, as were his eyes. He was the result of a union between Ms. Sevier's son and his Native American wife. They definitely were a good combination for children. Seth was gorgeous.

I was thankful that I'd already made dinner and I could afford to sit and stare at Seth. He seemed to like me, too. Well, either that or he was just being nice. But something about the smile he always wore when he saw me told me that he kind of fancied me.

I was so engrossed in watching him do his work that I didn't hear the front door open or Frank come in. I didn't even realize that he was watching me until he spoke.

All he said was, "Dinner ready?" But I knew. It was how he said it. The tone of his voice told me that he saw me staring at Seth and that I was in big trouble.

"Yes," I said as I scrambled to my feet. I walked over to him and kissed his cheek. He glared down at me and then rested his eyes on Seth, whose smile had disappeared.

"Um, all done," Seth said. Then he nodded at me and slipped out of the front door.

I rushed into the kitchen and fixed Frank a plate. His glower was glued to me as he walked into the kitchen and took a seat at the table. I stood next to the stove and stared at him. He picked up his fork and said, "You ain't gon' eat?"

I laughed nervously. "Yeah, I was just gonna fix me a plate."

He took a bite of food. "Yeah," he said through a mouthful of cream-style corn.

I fixed Aaron a plate and sat him at the table before fixing my own plate and sitting down across from Frank. We ate in silence. I kept my eyes cast downward, afraid to look at him.

I was engrossed in eating my peas when I heard Frank's fork clank loudly against the plate. I looked up to see that his plate was empty and he was staring at me. "You want seconds?" I asked.

"Yeah," he said in that same gruff voice that had greeted me when he first made it home. I fixed him another plate and had just reclaimed my seat when I saw his plate fly across the table. I tried to duck but I was too late. The plate full of food hit me square in the face and then went crashing to the floor. My face stung from the impact of the heavy porcelain. My nose began to bleed almost instantly. I looked up, my gaze clouded by corn, peas, and chicken grease, to see Frank standing from the table and freeing his belt from his pants. I quickly stood and stumbled backward, knocking my chair over.

Aaron, who had been undoubtedly startled by Frank's actions, was balling loudly. I tried to grab him, but Frank beat me to him. He grabbed him by the arm and dragged him to his small bedroom, shutting the door behind him. Aaron's cries were muffled as Frank returned to the kitchen. I turned to run away but slipped on the spilled food and fell the floor—the optimal position for what Frank had in mind.

He stood over me, his steel-toe boots surrounded by soupy corn and pea juice. "You just love to embarrass me, don't you?"

I began to whimper. "No...no, I don't."

He lifted the belt and brought it down with a loud "whack" against my shoulder. "Yeah, you do. I saw you staring at that half-breed boy. You want him, little sister? Huh? You been messing around with him? Cheating on me?"

I shook my head. "No. He's just a nice person, that's all."

A shadow came over his face. "What you trying to say? I'm not nice?"

"No...no, Frank. I wasn't saying that."

"You ungrateful little—" He interrupted his own words with another blow from the belt. This one landed right at the top of my head. I covered my head with my hands and felt the thick leather as it stung my knuckles. The beating went on until I could feel his sweat drip onto me.

Then he dropped the belt and knelt next to me. "You been doing that half-breed boy? Tell me the truth!" He screamed.

I was out of breath and nearly unconscious from the pain. "No," I said weakly.

He lifted my face and stared into my eyes. I gave him a pleading look and his expression seemed to soften a bit. "You better not be lying."

"I'm not," I said.

"Prove it."

I felt tears I didn't even know I had left as they began to crowd my eyes. The last thing I had the strength to do was to have sex with him the way he wanted me to. I shook my head. "I...I can't."

His eyes flashed with so much rage that if I'd had the strength, I would've grabbed my son, run from that house, and never looked back. He raised his fist and all I could do was to close my eyes and try to brace myself for the expected blow. His fist connected with my jaw and my head felt like it twisted all the way around on my neck. I slumped to the floor and he continued to pound me and when he got tired of hitting me, he kicked me. It became unbearable to think or even breathe and when I finally lost my battle with consciousness, the last thing I remember was Frank yanking my underwear off, mumbling something about taking what was his.

"G! G, wake up. Wake up. It was just a dream." Scott's voice sounded distant—almost as if I was imagining it. When I became aware of myself, I was still in bed, rolled up in the fetal position. My throat was sore—evidence that I had been screaming. I was trembling and the sheets beneath me felt wet and cold.

"Oh, no," I moaned. I smelled the familiar odor and knew that I had wet myself.

"G...G, it's okay. Stay here, alright. Don't move," Scott said. Then he left our bed. I heard him turn on the faucet in the bathroom. The sound of water filling the tub seemed to sooth me a bit. I was still lying in the bed, rolled into a tight ball when Scott gently began to undress me. I flinched at his touch.

"G, it's me, darlin'. It's Scotty. I'm not going to hurt you," he said softly.

My body was still rigid as he struggled to undress me. It took him much longer than it should have because of my body's lack of cooperation, but he finally rid me of my nightgown and underwear then lifted me from the bed and gently lowered me into the warm water. I relaxed almost instantly. I looked up at him through tears as he washed me.

"Frank did that, too," I said softly.

Scott stopped washing me and looked me in the eye. "He did what?"

"He washed me—after I woke up."

"After you woke up?"

I nodded.

After he beat me unconscious then raped me, he left me on the kitchen floor. I lay there for three days before I regained consciousness, or at least that's what Frank told me. I woke up feeling stiff, my head throbbing and my stomach lurching. The smell of urine hit me before I opened my eyes. When I was finally able to sit up, I saw that I was lying in a pool of urine. Dried blood left an outline on the floor where my head had rested.

Frank was sitting at the kitchen table holding Aaron in his lap. When he saw that I was awake, Aaron bolted from Frank's lap and hugged me tightly around the neck. He kissed my swollen lips and said, "Mommy hurt. Daddy hurt Mommy."

I looked up at Frank who wore a sheepish expression.

I closed my eyes and hugged Aaron back. "Mommy's okay," I lied.

"You get enough rest? You been sleep for three days," Frank said cheerily.

All I could do was nod—afraid that a single word would set him off. I struggled to get to my feet, but dizziness prevented it. Frank rushed to my aid, helping me to my feet then to one of the kitchen chairs. "You hungry?" he asked as he kissed my forehead.

I shook my head. "I need to take a bath. I...I smell."

"Okay, wait here," he said.

I held Aaron in my lap as I waited for Frank to return. I inspected him for any signs that Frank had taken his anger out on him while I was unconscious. My stomach dropped when I saw the bruises on his back. I knew then that I had to go. I had to get away from him for Aaron's sake if not for my own. I just had to figure out how I was going to do it.

When Frank returned to the kitchen he took Aaron and sat him on the floor. "Don't move," he said sternly.

The fear in Aaron's little eyes was more than I could bear. "Come on," Frank said as he took my arm and helped me from the kitchen to the bathroom. I stared at my reflection in the partially fogged-up bathroom mirror. Bruises covered nearly every inch of me. Frank's handprints were wrapped around my neck. My whole body ached.

Frank helped me into the tub and washed me. He even kissed my bruises and apologized for losing his temper with me. The only thing running through my mind was that I had to figure out a way to leave him. I had to get away before he killed me or worse, before he killed my son.

The look in Scott's eyes when I finished recounting that day so far in the past was a mixture of empathy and rage. He resumed washing me in silence. Was he angry at me for being so messed up? For having such a horrible past? My tears came before I could stop them. I was losing him. I was losing my family. If I lost them, what would I have left?

"It's okay, G. It's okay. I promise everything will be okay," Scott assured me.

I shook my head, flinging tears and snot in the process. "No, you're angry at me. You…you're tired of me."

He held my face in his hands. "G, is that what you think?"

"It's true. I'm a burden to you," I whimpered.

Scott took me in his arms, holding my wet body against his. "No, no, G. No, honey. No, I'm not angry with you. I'm angry with Frank.

I *hate* him for what he did to you. If I had my way, I'd make him pay. I'd shoot him down like a deer in the woods."

"I'm sorry. I'm so sorry."

He tightened his arms around me. "G, you have nothing to be sorry for. You were a child when you met him. He took advantage of you, of your trust. You did *nothing wrong*."

I closed my eyes and let him comfort me, because I needed his comfort more than anything else. He held me until the water grew cold and then he lifted me from the tub and took me to bed. I fell into a dreamless sleep and slept until late into the next morning.

17

"NOT LOOKIN'"

I was sitting in my car outside Rodney Kemp's apartment building, thinking about my life—past and present. I wondered if I was losing my mind and if so, would I ever find my way back? Rodney Kemp hadn't said so much as the word "boo" to me since our first little confrontation. He was even careful not to look my way. Was it because what Scott had said was true? Was he really not Frank Freeman? Had I made it all up in my head? Or was he actually afraid of me, of what I knew about him? He was a pedophile and I doubt if he was reformed. Maybe he was afraid I'd reveal his secrets.

But that really didn't make any sense. Frank had never been afraid of me. That is, until the day I left him. And that was only because I was holding his baseball bat over my head, ready to beat his brains out. But I held no weapon and other than what I knew of his past, I was no threat to him, was I?

The same question kept rolling over and over in my mind: Is he Frank? Is Rodney Kemp really Frank Freeman? Is he?

Is he?

I had to know—*needed* to know. As I sat there with my eyes fixed on his front door, I wondered what was inside. Was my answer behind that door? If I'd truly found him, would it ease my mind? Would the nightmares cease?

I closed my eyes and took several deep breaths before leaving the parking lot and driving home.

***

Weeks passed and no more memories came. No more dreams, no more nightmares. Maybe it was truly over. I hoped so. My family was returning to its normal rhythm—school, work, chores, church, family time. The sense of normalcy felt so refreshing. My children were wearing smiles again. My husband was able to sleep in peace, and things at work were uneventful.

I was still watchful of Rodney Kemp—but from afar. I even decreased my visits to his apartment building. I was finding it easier and easier to let go of my past, of what he'd done to me. Maybe Scott was right. In confronting the memories, I had finally freed myself of the pain.

I thought about my childhood more and more, though. I thought of my mother, whom I still loathed with all my heart. And I thought about my sister, Mo, whom I'd never stopped missing. Her number had checked out. It was really my sister on the other end of that call.

I'd lost count of the number of times I dialed that number but never pressed the send button. I wanted to talk to her so badly, to hear about her life. I hoped hers was better than mine had been, and I hoped she'd found the kind of love I'd found with Scott. I wondered if she had children. Was she saved? Did she go to church?

I even wondered about our mother. Did Mo keep in touch with her? There was so much I wanted to know, but deep inside of me I was afraid. I was afraid to reopen that door to my distant past. My memories of Frank's abuse had almost completely destroyed me. I surely didn't want to remember what my mother had subjected me to. And I was afraid that talking to Mo would bring on an avalanche of forgotten pain. I just couldn't risk it. Not now. Not when things were going so much better.

I looked over at Scott, who was manning the grill. I settled into my lawn chair and watched my children as they rode their horses through the field behind our house. It was harvest time and this was how Scott celebrated every year—with a cookout for the farm workers and their families. I smiled at the group of men and women who were huddled around picnic tables, drinking sodas and lemonade. It felt good to be normal again. Even Lee's constant stare didn't bother me. Nothing could shake me from this happiness. Nothing and no one.

***

"Be careful of the vows you make whether in your mind or with your mouth. Are you God that you can say what the future holds? Don't fool yourself. Only one is all knowing and it's not you!" Those words were spoken by an old preacher long ago. He was my father-in-law's father, Reverend Farris Grant. He was a short, stocky man with a huge voice. You couldn't ignore him or his words if you wanted to.

His words played over and over in my mind as I sat outside Rodney Kemp's apartment. I had vowed not to let anyone and anything shake my happiness. And I hadn't for a while. But then the memories returned. Not huge ones, but memories nonetheless. Memories of the torturous abuse I suffered towards the end of my time with Frank. He grew so mean to me and to Aaron. It was as if he knew I planned to leave him someway and somehow, and he was determined to punish me for even having the desire to escape him.

I stared at the door of the apartment and thought about how helpless and alone I'd felt knowing that Ms. Sevier must have heard what went on in that duplex. The walls weren't thick enough to muffle my screams or Aaron's cries. She'd heard it, I was sure of that. She'd heard it and she hadn't lifted a finger to help. No one ever helped. No matter where we lived or who our neighbor was. No one ever helped. In the end, I had to help myself. Just like today.

It was the week of Thanksgiving and I'd overheard Rodney Kemp telling one of the volunteers that he was visiting family out of town. He'd be gone for the entire week. The first thought that entered my mind was that I would finally have a chance to get into his apartment. I would finally be able to see who he really was once and for all.

I watched the apartment for several hours on Monday and Tuesday, making sure he was really gone before I made my move. There were no signs of life those two days and on this day, Wednesday, I was ready to check things out. But how would I get in there? I wasn't a criminal. I didn't know how to jimmy a lock. Should I break a window? Wouldn't someone hear me? Maybe the door was unlocked.

I laughed at my own thoughts. Talk about *ridiculous*. Here I was sitting in my car, trying to figure out how to break into someone's home. Me—the wife of a preacher's son, a mother, and a decent member of society—planning a break-in. I shook my head and at the same time, seemed to shake some sense back into myself. I started my car, put it in reverse and just as I was taking my foot off of the brake, I saw a curtain move in the window to apartment six. And for a brief, fleeting moment, I saw a face—a little girl's face.

18

"HE THINK I DON'T KNOW"

Had I imagined it? Did I really see her? Her frightened eyes seemed to beckon me, and almost mechanically, I shut my car off, pulled the key from the ignition, and opened my door. I climbed out of the car and slowly made my way to apartment six, to the little girl whose small face reminded me of my own face so many years ago.

I held my hand up to knock on the door and then a thought hit me: *what if she's just his daughter?* What if this is her home and she's supposed to be here? But then again, she looked to be no more than eight or nine-years-old. She shouldn't be in there alone.

What if she's not alone?

What if he's in there? What if he's been in there all the time? After all, I hadn't been watching the apartment 24-7. He could very well be in there. How would I explain my intrusion if he was?

Tell him you want to invite him to Thanksgiving dinner. Yes, that's it!

With a new plan in mind, I took a deep breath and knocked lightly at the door. My knocks were met with silence. I knocked again—no answer. *She's in there. I saw her*, I thought.

The woman in apartment five popped her foam roller-covered head out of her door and said, "He ain't there. Been gone all week."

"Do you know him?" I asked.

She shook her head. "Not really. He ain't all that friendly."

"What about his little girl? Does he leave her by herself a lot?"

The woman frowned. "He ain't got no little girl. He lives alone."

I turned back to the window where I'd seen the face. Had I really imagined it? I turned to leave. "Thank you," I said to the lady.

She shut her door and I stood on the sidewalk and wondered if I was losing my mind. She seemed so real. But, was she? I turned to take one last look at the apartment and I saw it again, the lightest flutter of the curtain…and the face. *Her* face.

I rushed back to the door. "Sweetheart, are you in there alone?" I said.

Silence.

"Sweetheart, I won't hurt you. I want to help you. Is your dad in there?"

More silence.

Then I made a decision. Even if she was his child, she shouldn't be in there alone. So I rushed to my car and dialed 911.

About ten minutes later, a sheriff's deputy's car pulled into the parking space next to mine. Deputy Arliss Grant, Scott's first cousin, stepped out of the vehicle and greeted me with, "Hey, G. You the one who called?"

I nodded. "Yes. There's a little girl in there alone. She can't be more than eight or nine."

He raised his blond eyebrows. "How'd you find her?"

I hesitated, and then said, "I work with the man that lives here. I came to invite him to dinner and then I saw the girl in the window."

"How you know she's alone?"

He was beginning to irritate me with the questions. "No one's answering the door—not even her. Something's wrong."

Arliss nodded and then walked up to the door and knocked a couple of times. His knocks went unanswered. I watched as he pressed his ear to the door for a moment. Then he turned to me and said, "Don't sound like no one's in there, G."

"I *saw* her, Arliss. I think she needs help."

Arliss gave me *the look*. The one everyone seemed to give me these days. The "you are out of your mind" look. Any other day, I would've agreed with him. But not today. I knew what I saw. I was not crazy. That girl was in there and I felt in my spirit that she needed help.

He jingled his keys in his hand and looked from me to the door as if he was trying to figure out what to do next.

"Can't you just get the landlord to unlock the door so you can check it out? Just to be safe. If it's nothing, then it's nothing," I said.

Arliss shrugged. "I guess that'd be okay. Wait here. I'll see if I can get the landlord."

Arliss went back to his car and I waited by the door. Like so many properties in town, there was no onsite manager. The complex was run by a leasing company. It took him twenty minutes to reach the landlord, but he finally did. We both stood by the door as the annoyed little red-headed woman unlocked the door to the apartment. Arliss slowly opened the door and stuck his head inside. The place was dark and silent. Not so much as a dripping faucet could be heard.

"I can't believe I'm doing this," Arliss muttered. Then he turned to me and said, "Stay here, G."

I nodded and stood there anxiously tapping my foot and silently praying that I hadn't lost what was left of my mind. *Please God, don't let me have imagined her.*

I wrapped my arms around my body and leaned in the door and peered into the darkness. I could make out the living room furniture and a small TV. It smelled musty and stuffy—like the windows had never been opened.

I felt the landlord's eyes on me and pulled myself out of the doorway. I wanted to go inside and look for her myself. I wanted to pull her to safety, and then I wanted to search for any signs of Rodney being Frank. I wanted to do something, *anything* besides stand and wait.

"Arliss, do you see her?" I called into the apartment.

No answer.

"Arliss!" I called again.

"Give me a minute, G. I'm still looking," he finally replied, annoyance in his voice.

"O…okay."

I leaned against the side of the building and closed my eyes. If I had imagined the girl, if she didn't really exist, I was doomed. Scott would probably have me admitted to a mental institution. I'd only be allowed to see my children under supervision. My life would be over, but who could blame him? I shut my eyes tightly. *Please let her be real…please let her be real…please let her be real…*

When I finally opened my eyes, I saw Arliss walking out of the apartment holding the girl's hand.

19

"LET NO MAN PUT ASUNDER"

I stood next to my car and watched the social worker as she belted the little brown girl into the front seat of her car.

"She says her name is Candace Little, and she's nine and a half. She's from Helena. We've already found her mother," Arliss said. He shook his head and added, "I can't imagine the things he did to her."

"I can," I said softly. I stared at the social worker's car as it drove away. "And you found her in a closet?" I asked, trying to wrap my mind around what he'd already told me twice.

He sighed. "Yeah. Evidently she slept there most of the time."

"And she said he picked her up on the side of the highway?" I asked. It was unreal, just unreal to think that my fate had been met by another little girl.

Arliss nodded. "Yeah, she was walking to school one morning and he offered her a ride. She told him 'no' because she didn't know him. He jumped out of his car and grabbed her. That was four months ago. We found pictures in there, too. Of other little girls. We're gonna try to match them up with some of the missing girls in

NamUs."

I frowned. "You think he's done this more than once?"

"Sure of it. He was too good at hiding it. He knows what he's doing. Now, we just need to find him, whoever he is," Arliss said as he rubbed his forehead.

"What do you mean, 'whoever he is'?"

"Well, we know he's not really Rodney Kemp and he's got about seven different ID's in there with seven different names on them. But we'll get him. The FBI's been called in, too."

I nodded and then a thought—a horrible thought occurred to me. "Do you think he killed those other girls, Arliss?"

"I'm sure of it, G. You just saved that little girl's life."

I shook my head. "No, God did that. He led me here, to her."

"Yeah, well, if you hadn't been obedient, we might've never found her."

I shrugged. "I guess you're right."

Arliss smiled at me. "You're a hero, G. Take it as it is, and soak it all up."

Before I could answer him, Scott pulled up in his truck. I looked at Arliss. "I called him," he said.

I allowed myself to smile for the first time that day as I walked to his truck. He stepped out, and I noticed all three of my children sitting in the bed. "Hey!" I called to them.

"Hey, mama," they said almost in unison.

I stopped in my tracks when I saw the look on Scott's face. There was no smile, no warmness in his eyes. He was angry.

"Scott—" I began, but when Scott clutched my arm, I found it impossible to speak another word. He'd never touched me in that way, grabbed me, or been even remotely forceful towards me before.

"I'm taking you home, G," he said sternly.

"My car…"

He continued to steer me to the truck and once I was inside, closed the door behind me. He climbed into the driver's seat and said, "We'll get it tomorrow. I'm not worried about it. It's insured. I can replace it. I can't replace you."

I stared at him as he started the car and pulled off of the parking lot. Then I shifted my eyes from him to the window beside me. I watched the trees and houses as we passed by them. It was getting dark outside, indicating that I'd been away from home for the better part of the day. It never occurred to me that I hadn't called home to check on Scott or the kids or to let them know I was okay. I could see why he'd be angry with me for being so inconsiderate, but when I saw that girl, Candace, she had been my one and only concern. Hadn't I done the right thing? Arliss said I'd saved her life.

When we made it home, Scott sent the kids to their rooms and directed me to the living room. My stomach began to grumble and I realized I hadn't had a bite to eat since breakfast. After downing a piece of toast and a glass of orange juice, I'd headed to Rodney Kemp's apartment complex. Now it was inching towards dinnertime and my empty stomach was full of complaints.

Scott heard it, too. "Stay here. I'll be right back," he ordered.

I did as I was told, knowing that this wasn't the time to argue with him. A few minutes later, he returned with a plate of the Thanksgiving dinner I'd finished preparing the night before and a can of soda. He placed the food before me on the coffee table and took a seat across from me in an accent chair. As he sat quietly with his elbows on his knees and his head in his hands, I felt like crying. Even in his anger towards me, his first instinct was to take care of me.

I picked up the plate and ate the food pretty quickly. It wasn't until I finished the last bite that he spoke.

"I can't do this anymore, G," he said as he looked up me, his elbows still on his knees, his fingers dug deeply into his thick hair.

I set the plate down on the table and stared at him. "Do…do what?" Was he leaving me? Taking my children? *No.*

He closed his eyes and I saw a single tear roll down his cheek. "I can't be the only one on this marriage."

"Scott—"

He held up his hand and straightened his posture as if he'd found a new supply of strength and resolve. "No, G. I want you to listen to me."

"O...okay."

"What you did today was foolish and reckless. It was dangerous, G. *Very* dangerous. Arliss says they think that guy is a serial killer."

I scooted to the edge of the sofa. "I know, Scott. I just—"

"No, G. Listen!"

I jumped. He'd never raised his voice at me before. I settled against the back of the sofa and shut my mouth.

He continued to speak. "You could've been hurt, or worse than that, you could've been killed, G. What would me and the kids do if something like that happened?"

"I'm sorry," I said weakly.

He ignored my apology. "But the worst thing is that you lied to me. You said you were going in to work. I had no idea you were at that apartment building until Arliss called me. You could have disappeared. Me and the kids might never have known what happened to you!"

I stood and walked over to him. I cautiously placed my hand on his shoulder. "I'm sorry, Scotty. I really am. I wasn't thinking when

I did it. It…it was something I felt I had to do, and I knew you wouldn't understand."

He stood to face me. "Understand? What I don't understand is how easy it was for you to lie to me and how it never crossed your mind to call home and tell me where you were."

"Scott—"

"I love you, G. I love you more than anyone else on this earth. I love you with all of my heart and soul. I really do. But I can't compete with your memories or your past or your determination to destroy what we have. I can't."

His words sliced through me. "Scott, I can't change my past."

"I know that. But you can choose to let it go…to let *him* go."

"I'm trying to do that. I really am."

"No you're not. You went over there today because you believed Rodney was Frank—not to rescue that little girl. You're still chasing him—why, I don't know. Am I not enough?"

My mouth fell open. "Is that what you think? Of course you are! You are more than enough. You are everything to me, Scotty!" I forced my arms around him and squeezed him tightly. "I wasn't chasing *him*. I just had to know the truth. I had to know if it was Frank or not."

He gently pushed me away from him. "But why? Why did you

have to know? You *know* that I love you. You *know* that the kids love you. Why can't that be enough, G?"

I tried to capture his gaze, but he wouldn't look at me. "*It is*. It is enough. I can't explain it. I was compelled to go there. I think God sent me there to help that girl. Now, I can go on. Things will be better now. I promise." I hugged him again.

"Was he Frank?" he asked.

"I really don't know. Could be, but it doesn't matter anymore. I'm done chasing the past."

He slowly rubbed his hand up and down my back. "I wish I could believe you, G."

"You can. I promise. I'll get counseling…whatever it takes to prove it to you."

He backed away a little and looked me in the eye. "You will?"

I nodded. "I will. I'm sorry for putting you through so much. I love you, Scotty. I love you so much."

He pulled closer. "I love you, too."

20

"TESTIMONY"

I sat in the group counseling session silently praying for the women sitting around me. They came from all walks of life. Some were residents in our shelter, having escaped abusive relationships. Others were seeking solace and comfort for situations that they were still involved in. Some were well-to-do with nice homes and successful husbands. Others shared run-down homes or small apartments with their boyfriends. But the group that tugged hardest at my heartstrings was the young girls, the teenagers who were being abused by boyfriends or relatives.

I knew their pain more than anyone else's. I understood their downcast eyes and their slumped posture of shame. I empathized with them. I mourned for their youth. I mourned for their uncertain futures.

I was a part of two counseling groups—this one, the domestic abuse group, and another for survivors of child abuse and molestation. My time with Frank fell into both categories, making me a unique case. In addition to that, I would eventually have to confront the molestation I suffered at the hands of one of my mother's friends and her physical and emotional abuse towards me.

Thinking of it all was intimidating and often times it left me wondering if it was even possible for me to heal from so much. But whenever that thought entered my mind, I remembered that I believed in God and that He believed in me. That's all I ever needed to remember.

I let my eyes drift from face to face. Beautiful women surrounded me. Beautiful women with horrible stories of abuse. I had to wonder how there could be so many evil people walking the earth. How could so many people be so willing to hurt the ones they are supposed to love? Frank always said he loved me. Even as he was beating me sometimes he'd say it. Once he told me he hit me *because* he loved me. "Spare the rod and spoil the child," he'd said. I remember wondering how I could be a child one moment and his woman the next. It was so confusing for me back then. But he was all I had, and that life was all I knew.

It became normal to me.

And at some point in time, I came to love him as a father *and* a lover. It's strange to think of it that way, but that's what he was to me—*a father and a lover*. A protector and an abuser. He was everything good and everything bad all rolled into one. It wasn't until the bad began to outweigh the good that I decided to break free.

I shut my thoughts off and turned my attention to Renata, a sixteen-year-old girl who was in an abusive relationship with an older man. A flood of tears spilled from her small, brown eyes as she recounted her most recent experience of physical abuse. I listened to the hopelessness she expressed as she explained that it was her fault. I'd felt the same way when Frank would hurt me. It had to be my fault. As a child, don't you get spankings when you misbehave? What was different about a lover hitting you? That's how a lot of us think.

Us.

The abused.

When the session was over, I made sure to give Renata my phone number for emergencies or if she just needed to talk. Heaven had saved my life once. Maybe I could do the same for Renata one day.

As I climbed into my car, I thanked God for these new women in my life and for their stories. I prayed His protection over them—over all of us. And then I drove home to my husband, the love of my life, and as I curled up next to him in our bed, I thanked God for him, too.

***

It seemed I spent all of my time talking about the one thing I'd spent years avoiding—Frank Freeman. In addition to the group sessions, I had private sessions with Connie, the shelter's on-site counselor, twice weekly. It was hard at first, but as time went on, it became very therapeutic. It felt good to get these things off of my chest and I was glad not to be bombarding Scott with it anymore.

"Gina, so many women stay—afraid of leaving. How did you manage to break free? How did you find the courage to leave Frank?" Connie asked.

I sighed and shifted in my seat as I thought about those events so many years ago. The fearful determination I'd felt at that time was still so fresh in my mind. "When he started abusing Aaron, I knew I had to leave. I was very afraid. I'd tried to leave him, and failed once before. This time, I had to worry about Aaron's well-being, too. I wasn't sure if we would make it, but I knew I had to try," I said.

Connie leaned forward in her chair. "He'd begun to abuse Aaron?"

I nodded and choked back tears of anger. "He would hit him or push him when Aaron got in his way or on his nerves. He'd make him sit in one spot for hours sometimes because he didn't want to be bothered with him. And then—" I stopped short of saying the one thing I never wanted to remember.

"Gina, there's nothing you can share with me that will go any further than this office. But, if you feel uncomfortable, we can stop for now."

I shook my head and gave up the battle with my tears. I let them fall from my eyes as I clutched my hands tightly in my lap. "No, I need to say this. I need to get it off of my chest."

She handed me a tissue and said, "Okay, I'm listening."

"One day I was in the bathroom and it was only for a minute or so. I'd learned not to leave Aaron alone with him, but I thought he'd be okay for that short while. When I went back into the living room, Aaron was in Frank's lap and Frank's pants were unzipped.

"I rushed over to them and snatched Aaron out of his lap. I asked Frank what was going on. Well, actually I screamed it. Frank's answer was to stand up with this smug look on his face and walk away. I followed him with Aaron on my hip and I demanded an answer. Frank turned around and back-handed me and then he went into our bedroom and shut the door. That was it—no answer, but I knew he'd done something to Aaron. I just knew it."

"And that's when you decided to leave?"

I nodded. "I knew I had to. I couldn't let him molest my baby. So, I devised a plan…"

I knew that the only way I'd be able to safely leave him would be to weaken him in some way. I couldn't plan to do it when he was gone to work, because he managed to pop in throughout the day to check on us. I never knew when he was coming home for lunch or one of his breaks. It was a different time every day. So I'd have to weaken him. That was the only way.

One night, I made sure to fix him his favorite dinner. I smiled and acted like nothing was wrong that whole night—waited on him hand and foot. I put Aaron to bed extra early and wore the sexiest thing I could find. When bedtime came, I acted like I couldn't keep my hands off of Frank. I did my best to wear him out—and it worked. Before I knew it, he was knocked out. I listened to him snore for thirty minutes before I made my move.

I slipped out of bed and dressed quietly. I dragged the duffel bag I'd packed from Aaron's closet and slipped Aaron's shoes on him. I knew I'd need to make a quick escape. I left Aaron in his bed and then I went to the living room closet where Frank kept a baseball bat I'd never seen him use. I took the bat to the bedroom and stood over Frank with it.

For a brief moment, I began to have second thoughts. He was lying there on his side asleep, looking so peaceful. I wondered if I was doing the right thing. Then he stirred a little and in a knee-jerk reaction, I slammed the bat against his shoulder. He groaned loudly and moved to sit up, but the bat crashed against his jaw, sending him back to the bed. I swung that bat over and over and over again. I hit him so many times that I quickly lost count. I could've easily killed him. I had a right to, didn't I?

That was the question I asked myself over and over again as he lay writhing and moaning on the bloodied sheets of our bed. Don't I have the right to kill him? For me? For Aaron?

He begged me to stop. He begged me for mercy. Mercy? Did he deserve mercy from me? Had he ever shown me any?

I lifted the bat high over my head. No, he had never shown me mercy. Not when I was twelve—not now. No, he didn't deserve mercy from me. God would have to forgive me, because I was going to kill him, and I felt absolutely no remorse about it. None.

The bat trembled in my hands. Rage filled me from top to bottom. I hated this man who'd hurt me so many times, who'd brutalized my child. He'd hurt my little boy. He needed to die.

It was right.

It was justice.

I held the bat above my head as I leaned over and spit in his bloody face. As I prepared to land the final blow, movement in the doorway caught my eye. Little Aaron was standing there staring at me with drowsy, curious eyes. And I knew I couldn't do it. I couldn't kill his father with him watching.

So I dropped the bat with a loud clang and took Frank's wallet from the dresser before leaving that house on foot while carrying my boy in my arms. I never looked back. I never went back because God sent an angel to me a few days later.

"Scott," Connie said softly.

I smiled. "Yes, Scott was my angel. He still is."

She crossed her legs and looked at me for a moment, then said, "Do you think violence was really the answer? Could you have found another way to leave?"

"I suppose it wasn't. But I was very young back then—only

nineteen. At that time, it was the best plan I could come up with. And it worked. I lived, and I got away from him."

"Do you ever wish you'd killed him?"

I hesitated then said, "I do. God help me, there's not a day that goes by when I don't regret letting him live."

21

"BE HAPPY"

Scott walked back in from the porch and reclaimed his seat next to me on the couch. "That was Arliss checking on us," he said.

"How long are they gonna do this? It's starting to get old," I said.

"Until they catch Rodney Kemp or whoever he is. They just wanna make sure we're okay since you're the one who blew the lid off of this thing."

"Yeah, well, it's been weeks and I doubt he's worried about me. He's probably too busy trying to stay free. If they catch him, he's going away for a long time."

"Yeah, I know. Just humor them. At least they're being proactive about protecting you."

I shrugged. "I guess."

He wrapped his arm around my shoulder and pulled me close to him. "Therapy going okay?"

I nodded. "It really is. I feel better each day. How are you?"

He gave me a surprised look. "I'm good as long as you're good."

I smiled. "I'm better than good. I'm great as long as I have God and you."

He hugged me tightly and kissed my head. "Well, neither of us is going anywhere. I can guarantee that."

I laid my head on his shoulder. "Hmm, that's so good to know."

"You know, since the house is all secured, and the kids are already tucked in, I was thinking we could head on upstairs for a little quality time."

I raised my head and looked up at him. "Quality time? That sounds like an offer I can't refuse."

He stood from the sofa and took my hand in his. "Let's get on this, then. I'm more than ready."

I grinned as I took his hand and followed him through our house. "Aren't you always?"

***

I woke up the next morning to the smell of coffee brewing and what was undoubtedly bacon frying in a skillet. I smiled as I reached over and felt Scott's empty side of the bed. It was Saturday morning—the day Scott and the kids always cooked breakfast.

I sat up on the side of the bed and gazed across the room at my reflection in the mirror. I smiled at the mess of hair that often seemed too much for my head—or at least it did to me. But as the years rolled by, I'd come to realize my unruly hair was just another part of me. It was as much a part of me as my eyes, nose, and mouth. I stood up and inspected my full body. Once so frail and thin, I now wore the curves of a woman and a mother. I smiled again thinking of my sister Mo, who was curvy before she even hit puberty. She'd complained about her body—I'd envied it.

I wrapped my robe around me and stepped into a pair of plush slippers before heading downstairs to find the kitchen all abuzz with my worker-bee family. Everyone was doing their part: Aaron was frying the bacon, Shane was busy buttering a pan of biscuits, and little Serenity was setting the table. Scott was whipping up some of his signature scrambled eggs.

I plopped down on a chair and waited to be served. In no time, we were all sitting around the table with full plates in front of us as Scott said grace. We ate and laughed and talked about the day ahead.

"I know I saw one this morning, Dad. Can we go hunting today?" Aaron said, trying to convince Scott that he'd seen a deer just beyond the tree line behind our house.

Scott shook his head. "Son, deer season is over. We'd be breaking the law if we shot it."

"Come on. No one has to know. And anyway, I think it was a

doe," Aaron said, knowing that his father had an affinity to doe meat.

Scott's eyes lit up. "A doe?"

"Yes, sir. I mean, what if we were just doing some target practice and the deer just accidentally got shot?" Aaron suggested.

"Aaron! That's being dishonest. Your dad said no. Now leave it alone," I said.

"Well, G. We do need to get in some target practice…" Scott said slowly.

I shook my head. "I'm not bailing you two out if you get caught."

"Aw, Ma. Nobody's ever in our woods. Who's gonna catch us?" Aaron asked.

"Yeah, he's right," Scott said.

"What if Arliss comes through to do one of his checks? Then what? How am I gonna explain the gunfire coming from the woods?" I asked.

Scott raised his eyebrows. "Oh, didn't I tell you? They caught Rodney Kemp early this morning in Missouri. Arliss called before you woke up and let me know. So, no more security checks for us."

"Well, that's good to know. But you guys will still be breaking the law, and I want no part of it," I said as I stood and began clearing the table.

"So you won't be eating any deer meat?" Scott asked as he followed me to the sink.

"I didn't say *that*. But if the authorities happen to drop by, I'm pleading ignorance."

"Ok, kids, grab your coats, we're going hunt—I mean, shooting. We're going to shoot some tin cans near where Aaron saw the deer," Scott said with a devious look in his eye.

I rolled my eyes as all three kids bolted to their rooms in preparation for "shooting practice".

Just a few minutes later, Aaron and Shane raced to the back door with their rifles and waited for Scott. Serenity, the only one of the bunch who hadn't been issued a firearm, brought up the rear. Seconds later, Scott came back through the kitchen pulling on his thick camouflage jacket and kissed me on the cheek.

"We'll be back in a bit. Surely it won't take us long to shoot those cans," he said with a grin.

"It's a shame you can't just stay here. I was thinking about having more quality time with you," I whispered in his ear and then kissed his ear lobe.

"Kids, start heading out. I'll catch up with you guys. Don't shoot anything until I get there. Aaron's in charge," Scott said without taking his eyes off of me.

"Yes, sir," they all said in unison.

"As a matter of fact, Shane, leave your rifle. I'll bring it with me. I don't want you to be tempted," Scott added.

Shane let out a long "aw, man" before setting his gun on the kitchen table and following his siblings out the back door and shutting it behind them.

"You think it's a good idea to be sending them out alone like that?" I asked as Scott began to kiss my neck.

"Aaron's responsible enough to handle it. Besides, this won't take me long," he said as he shrugged out of his jacket.

"Um, Scotty, that's not the kind of thing a woman likes to hear."

"Think of it as an appetizer, the full meal will come later. I promise." With that, he lifted me from the floor and carried me to the kitchen table where the appetizer was just about to begin when we heard a knock at the door.

"Kids, I'm coming in a second," Scott yelled towards the door.

"Sweetie, you're making this sound worse and worse," I said as he turned his attention back to me.

"I'm kidding. It'll take me at least five seconds," he said.

"Five seconds is just not enough for me. Not gonna work," I said through a giggle.

"Sir?" A voiced from the other side of the door said. It was definitely not the voice of one of our children.

"Dang-it!" Scott said under his breath. "I forgot Lee was coming to do some work this morning. Rain check?"

"If you promise I can look forward to more than five seconds," I said as I slid from the table to my feet.

"Count on at least a full minute," he said as he opened the door. By then we were both laughing.

"Mr. Lee, you're right on time. Let me show you what I need you to do," Scott said cheerily.

I'd turned to leave the kitchen when I heard a sickening sound that stopped me in my tracks. It was a sound that was all too familiar to me. And before I turned around, I knew what had happened. It was the sound of a baseball bat cracking against my husband's skull.

22

"SHAKE DOWN"

The room started to spin as I watched my husband fall to the floor, his head bloodied by the bat. My first instinct was to rush to his side—to help him. I knelt beside him with dry eyes, trying to assess the damage Lee had done.

Lee.

My head snapped up and I looked at the man who'd hurt my husband. I stood to my feet and faced him and I saw him for the first time. I saw past the missing teeth and the leathered skin and the crooked nose. And I realized fully who he was. Rodney Kemp was an evil man who hurt young girls, but he wasn't Frank Freeman. *Lee* was Frank Freeman.

I felt my bladder spasm, threatening to release urine I didn't realize I was holding. I squeezed my legs together and shut my eyes tightly, hoping that when I opened them, I would no longer see Frank in Lee's eyes. Maybe this was just another nightmare. Maybe Frank wasn't standing in my kitchen wielding a baseball bat. Maybe Scott wasn't on the floor with a gash in his head.

I opened my eyes. Frank was still there. This was no dream.

"Frank," I said through a gasp.

"Cleo," he said with a sickening smile.

"*Why?*" was all I could say at that point.

He lifted the bat. "Remember this?"

My eyes travelled from his face to the bat. It was *the* bat. The same one I'd used to make my escape so many years ago. I nodded.

"You used it to hurt me once. I'ma use it to hurt you now," he said.

I looked down at Scott. "You already have. You hurt me over and over again."

"Not like I'm going to."

"What took you so long?"

He shrugged. "I was waiting to see if you'd recognize me, but you didn't. So I decided to make myself known."

"Then do what you came to do and leave before my children come back."

"No, I have plans for them, too. Especially that pretty little girl of yours. But first, I think we need to spend a little time together." He moved closer to me, lowered his head and sniffed my neck. "I sure have missed my little sister. I been looking for another one like you for years. Never could find one, though."

I felt my body begin to tremble with a combination of fear and rage. Had he molested other girls? Had he abused them, too? *I should've killed him when I had the chance.*

He reached around and grabbed my butt. "Having them mixed babies sure did thicken you up. Shoot!"

He smiled at my pained expression. "Don't worry. We ain't gon' do nothing we haven't done before lots of times. You remember how we used to love on each other all the time, Cleo?"

I turned my head as he tried to kiss me. He grabbed my face and turned it back towards his. "Hmm, I'm so glad I found you, little sister. At first I wasn't sure it was you. You know when I realized it *was* you?"

I closed my eyes as the tears finally began to fall.

"Do you?!" he demanded.

"No," I said, softly.

"It was that morning when I first saw you. I thought it was you, but you done thickened up so much, I wasn't sure. Then you and that white boy started loving each other right there at that table. I guess you thought I was gone, but I was right there at the window looking. I saw you making those faces you used to make for me. It burned me up to see that white boy getting what belongs to me!" He kicked Scott in the side. I felt my stomach lurch when I saw his body jerk in response.

"What do you want?!" I hissed.

"I want *you*, baby. Don't you know that? I want to get what's mine, and then I want to beat you like a dog with this bat, like you did me."

I dropped my head. "But my children. Your son..."

"Now you know I didn't never want no damn kids. I tell you what; I'll make it painless for the boys. Now as for the little girl, I'm taking her with me. If she's anything like you, she'll keep me happy for a very long time."

That's when it kicked in—the adrenaline that kicks in when a person's life is threatened. But it was actually hearing Frank's plans for my children that pushed me to move. I kneed him in the groin and as he doubled over, I ran from the kitchen towards the living room...to the gun cabinet. I nearly fell to pieces when I realized it was locked. *Damn, damn, damn!* I was always preaching to Scott about keeping that cabinet locked, and now I wished I'd kept my mouth shut.

What should I do? Almost instantly, a picture formed in my mind. *Shane's gun is on the kitchen table.* It was right there in the kitchen, only a few feet away. But so was Frank.

23

"MR. WRONG"

I stood frozen, unsure as to what my next move should be. If I went into the kitchen, there was no way I could avoid Frank. Besides, he probably had Shane's gun in his hands by now. I could run into the woods and get Aaron's gun, but that would put the kids in danger. I would be leading Frank right to them. There was a baseball bat in the living room closet, but it would be no match for Shane's gun if Frank indeed had it.

"Watchu doing, Cleo?" Frank's voice startled me. I turned around to find him standing behind me, holding the bat in one hand and Shane's gun in the other. A lump formed in my throat. *He's going to kill me.*

My hands seemed to move on their own as I picked up a lamp and threw it at the gun cabinet, shattering the thick glass doors. Why hadn't I thought of that before? *Just break the glass.* I grabbed a rifle and trained it on Frank. A smile spread across his face.

"I bet that thing ain't even loaded," he said with an amused look on his face.

"I bet it is," I said.

"So you gon' shoot me, Cleo?"

"Before I let you hurt my kids, I will."

He laughed. "You done moved from bats to guns, huh? That white boy in there got you thinking you tough now, I guess."

"That *white boy* taught me how to shoot a gun and he taught me well," I replied, holding the gun surprisingly steady.

Frank lifted Shane's rifle. "I can shoot, too, you know."

"Good, because you'll have to kill me if you think you are going to lay a finger on my children."

"It don't have to be this way, G. Can I call you that or is that only the white boy's pet name for you?"

I didn't answer him. He moved a little closer to me and I adjusted my finger on the trigger of my gun.

"You think you're something else, don't you? In your big white house with your white husband and your half-white kids. You think you are some big stuff. I guess I just ruined all this for you, didn't I? Since I killed your white boy."

I felt a pain shoot through my chest. When I'd checked Scott he was still breathing, it was shallow, but he was alive. Was he really dead now?

My face must've shown my concern because Frank said, "Oh, you didn't know? Yeah, he's gone. No more white boy for you."

I stared at him, checking his face for any signs he was lying. I found none. My heart ached for Scott. My head throbbed with the desire to kill Frank.

"So what we gon' do? Shoot each other? Leave your kids to find our bodies?" he asked.

"I don't plan on dying," I replied.

"Then what—"

Boom!

It wasn't until the smoke settled that I realized I'd pulled the trigger. The blood rapidly covering his shirt told me that I'd shot him in the stomach. He collapsed to the floor, dropping Shane's gun in the process. I rushed to pick it up then stood over Frank as he gurgled blood and moaned loudly.

"I guess you thought I was the same little girl you picked up on the side of the road all those years ago." I squatted beside him and brought my face close to his. "Well, you thought wrong."

I left him on the floor and went into the kitchen to Scott. I checked him. He was still breathing, thank God. But he didn't look good at all. I grabbed the kitchen phone and called 911. Then I sat down on the floor and held Scott's hand as I prayed for him. I closed my eyes and begged God to help him. And when I opened them, I saw Frank Freeman, his shirt soaked in blood, as he stumbled into the kitchen with the bat in his hand.

24

"IRREVERSIBLE"

I looked across the room where I'd dropped the guns by the door. There was no way I could reach them in time. It would be awhile before the police or the ambulance made it way out here in the boondocks. I'd just have to hope Frank collapsed from blood loss before he could beat me to death. It was a sad thought but it was true.

"You thought you killed me, didn't you?" he asked, his words slurred.

"I hoped I did," I said.

"I might die, but so will you," he said. Then he lifted the bat above his head and I closed my eyes. No sense in running. I couldn't leave Scott behind for him to finish him off. Then I heard a voice.

"Get away from my mama." It was Aaron.

I opened my eyes to see Aaron standing in the doorway leading from the kitchen to the living room with his rifle pointed at Frank— his father.

"Aaron, put the gun down. Where are your brother and sister?" I said softly.

"I told them to wait out in the woods when I heard a gun go off back here," he said, his eyes glued to Frank.

Frank stumbled a little as he turned to face Aaron. "You know who I am, boy?" he said, spitting blood with every syllable.

"Yeah, I do now," Aaron said matter-of-factly.

"Then you know I'm your daddy. You gon' shoot your daddy?"

"My daddy is on that floor. You ain't nobody to me," Aaron said as a single tear fell from his eye.

Frank laughed a hideous, gurgly laugh. Then he coughed and wheezed for a full minute before speaking again. "That white boy aint yo' daddy. That's my blood running through your veins."

"You used to hit my mama and you used to hit me. I remember and I hate you."

Frank's expression changed from one of amusement to one of surprise. "You can't remember that. Your mama been lying to you."

Aaron shook his head. "No, I remember."

"Then shoot me, you little bastard!" Frank said.

Aaron stared at him.

"I didn't think so. Living with this white boy got you all soft. If I had raised you, you'd be a real man. You ain't no more a man than your little sister. You just a little soft punk!" He turned to me and raised the bat over his head again.

I screamed but was powerless to stop what happened next. I watched in horror as Aaron pulled the trigger and shot his own father in the back.

25

"JUST FINE"

Frank fell to the floor almost instantly. I stared at the bat as it dropped to the floor beside him with a loud, vibrating clang. I didn't have to check his pulse or his breathing to know that he was gone. There was no light in his eyes as they stared up at the ceiling. Frank was dead. There was no doubt about that.

I could hear sirens growing closer and closer. "Give me the gun, Aaron," I said.

Aaron was staring at Frank, still holding the gun on him as if he was afraid he'd jump up from the floor any second, like the villain always does in a horror movie. But this wasn't a movie. This was reality. Frank was dead and Aaron had killed him.

I got to my feet and walked slowly over to Aaron. "Hand me the gun, baby."

Aaron looked at me with a blank expression on his face.

I reached for the gun. "Give me the gun and go back to the woods to your brother and sister."

He continued to stare wordlessly at me as if I was speaking a foreign language.

I placed my hands on his shoulders and shook him gently. "Aaron, give me the gun and go find your brother and sister. Stay out there until I come get you."

I caught the gun as he let it slip from his hand. "Aaron, go find your brother and sister. You guys stay out there until I come get you, okay?"

He nodded slowly and as he turned to leave, I added, "You weren't here, Aaron. You didn't shoot him." I stared him in the eye to be sure he understood. I could see a flicker of confusion in his eyes before he raised his eyebrows slightly and said, "Yes, ma'am."

He left the house and I watched him through the kitchen window as he first trotted, then ran full-speed into the woods. I could see Shane and Serenity standing just beyond the tree line as Aaron grabbed their hands and pulled them with him. Then I took Aaron's gun, fired a shot into the air, and collapsed beside Scott. *There, the residue is on my hands, now. I shot him—not Aaron.* I wrapped my arms around Scott and listened to the ambulance and police cars as they rushed into our driveway.

***

I sat next to Scott's bed, holding his hand and thanking God that he was okay. It had been touch and go for a few days. He'd suffered a fractured skull with swelling in his brain that threatened to cause brain damage, but he'd emerged the same Scott we all knew and loved. He was on his way to a full recovery and I was so grateful for that.

After answering tons of questions, I'd finally convinced the authorities that I'd killed Lee Parker after he attacked Scott in an attempt to burglarize us. They now believed that I shot him once to stop the attack on Scott and a second time when he tried to attack Scott again. It wasn't that hard of a sell considering Scott's condition.

I'd decided to wait awhile before I told Scott the whole truth. He was unconscious when Aaron shot Frank in the back. So, as far as he knew, what I said was true. He didn't even know that Lee was really Frank Freeman. I'd tell him eventually, but right now, the most important thing was his recovery. The rest would come later.

The kids were doing okay. Aaron had grown very quiet, and I knew he'd need someone to talk to. I'd get him the help he needed to cope with what happened. I'd asked God for forgiveness and I'd repented, but I'd never regret lying to protect him. It was the only way I could safeguard his future. It *had* to be done.

I smiled over at Scott and squeezed his hand. He'd saved my life once when he rescued me from a little Oklahoma diner with nothing but pennies in my pocket and no place to lay my head. He'd been my angel. Now, I'd return the favor. I'd saved his life. So had Aaron.

I closed my eyes as a feeling of peace came over me. *Everything will be okay, now. I know it will.*

He returned my smile. "I love you, G," he said softly.

"I love you, too, Scotty."

EPILOGUE

It took me months of therapy—group and one-on-one—to get to this point. I sighed as I gazed out the window at the house. I held my phone in my hand and took a deep breath, then I dialed the number, but I couldn't press the send button.

"You can do it," Scott said as he rested his hand on my arm.

I looked at him. "I don't know that I can."

He gave me a reassuring smile. "I know you can."

I turned my attention back to the house. It was a neat brick house with a shiny SUV in the driveway. I'd just watched a hulking man and two teenage boys leave. And then I'd seen her standing in the doorway with a baby on her hip, smiling as she waved goodbye to them. She was just as beautiful as I remembered. She was my sister.

I stared at her as I sat wondering if I was really ready to see her face to face. Could I deal with the memories of my childhood? I'd run from them for so long and it still hurt to discuss them in therapy. What would it do to me to talk to Mo?

She'd been my protector and basically a mother to me when our mother refused to care for us. For a long time, she was all I had—

then I left. Was she angry at me for disappearing? Had she been looking for me all this time? She'd called before. Was she still trying to find me?

I stared at the numbers on the screen of my phone until they began to blur. Then I watched as she turned to go back into her house and I hit the send button.

"Hello," she answered breathily.

"Um, is this Mona-Lisa Dandridge?" I asked.

"Yes, who's calling?"

"This is Gina Grant. You called me awhile back, asking about your sister."

There was silence for a moment. Then she softly said, "I remember. Y...you said you didn't know her."

I closed my eyes. "I'm sorry about that. I...I lied. I wasn't ready then, but I am now. Is it possible for me to meet with you in person?"

"Ready for what? I don't understand—"

I interrupted her as my anxiousness overwhelmed me. "Mo, I'm right outside your house. I'm...I'm sitting in my car. I'd like to see you."

She didn't answer. The next thing I saw was her front door as it burst open. She rushed directly to my car with the baby bouncing on *her wide hip. As she stood and stared at me through my window, tears began to fall from her eyes.*

I opened the door and stood in front of her, my own eyes filling with tears.

"Cleo," she said. "It's you, isn't it? I'd know you anywhere."

I nodded as Scott climbed out of the car and walked around to us. He stood beside me with a huge grin on his face. "This is my husband," I said.

Mo glanced at him and said, "Good, then he can hold my baby." She handed the baby to him and grabbed me, pulling me into the tightest, warmest hug I've ever felt. We hugged and cried and laughed as we touched each other's faces and kissed each other's cheeks. And with those gestures, we said all that needed to be said: I love you. I missed you. I'm glad I found you.

And for the first time in more than eighteen years, we were whole again—my sister and me.

For more information about missing children, go to:

www.missingkids.com

For more information about domestic violence, go to:

www.domesticviolence.org

For more information about the author, go to:

http://adriennethompsonwrites.webs.com

Get connected!

Follow Adrienne on Twitter: **https://twitter.com/A_H_Thompson**

Like **Author Adrienne Thompson** on Facebook!

Contact Adrienne via email: **tapestrywriter@gmail.com**

Excerpt from *Been So Long 2 (Body and Soul)*

Coming in 2013

I was sitting on the side of my bed reading a book when I heard the soft knock. I looked up at Wasif who stood in the doorway with his hands in the pockets of his slacks, his eyes downcast.

He sighed heavily. "Look, I'm sorry for what I said the other night. It was not the right time or the right thing to say in that situation."

I stared at him for a moment and then returned my attention to my book.

"Mo, we've got to have some type of relationship for the boys' sake."

I stood and walked towards the door, sliding past him. I could hear him following me as I made it to my destination—the front door. I opened it and stepped to the side.

He stood in front of me. "So this is what it's going to be like from now on? You're gonna keep giving me the silent treatment? Did what I said really upset you that much?"

I raised my eyes to meet his. "No, but I don't have time for whining and complaining from grown men, that's all."

He backed up a little. "Whining and complaining? Wow, you really are a cold-hearted woman. Forget it, I prefer the silent treatment."

"Good."

He stepped towards the door and hesitated. "You know, Mo. I wish I knew what about Corey Sanders made it so easy for you to throw me away. I wonder about that all the time."

I sighed. "Well, I guess it's the same reason you married another woman and made me your mistress."

He turned and looked me in the eye. "I've apologized for that. I tried to make up for it. I left her, remember? My father hasn't talked to me in a year."

"And that's my fault? You made those decisions. You made *all* of those decisions—including marrying that woman!" I said, raising my voice.

His shoulders sagged. "Mo...look, I didn't mean for this to be an argument. I...I just wanted you to understand."

I placed my hands on my hips and leaned forward. "Understand what, Wasif? What the hell are you talking about?"

"That..." he paused, a pensive look on his face.

"What?" I asked, my patience running thin.

"Nothing. I gotta go. I'll be back next week."

I shrugged. "Fine. Whatever."

I closed the door and leaned against it, wondering why after three years, we were rehashing the past and why did it make me feel so bad?

www.ingramcontent.com/pod-product-compliance
Lightning Source LLC
Chambersburg PA
CBHW070039260626
47159CB00005B/2087